Take Me © 2017 Lucy Leroux

All rights reserved under the International and Pan-American Copyright Conventions. No part of this book may be reproduced or transmitted in any form or by any means, electronic or mechanical, including photocopying, recording, or by any information storage and retrieval system, without permission in writing from the publisher.

This is a work of fiction. Names, places, characters and incidents are either the product of the author's imagination or are used fictitiously, and any resemblance to any actual persons, living or dead, organizations, events or locales is entirely coincidental.

Warning: the unauthorized reproduction or distribution of this copyrighted work is illegal. Criminal copyright infringement, including infringement without monetary gain, is investigated by the FBI and is punishable by up to 5 years in prison and a fine of $250,000.

❦ Created with Vellum

TITLES BY LUCY LEROUX

The Complete Singular Obsession Series
Making Her His
Confiscating Charlie, A Singular Obsession Novelette
Calen's Captive
Stolen Angel
The Roman's Woman
Save Me, A Singular Obsession Novella
Take Me, A Singular Obsession Prequel Novella
Trick's Trap
Peyton's Price

The Complete Spellbound Regency Series
The Hex, A Free Spellbound Regency Short
Cursed
Black Widow
Haunted

The Rogues and Rescuers Series
Codename Romeo
The Mercenary Next Door
Knight Takes Queen
The Millionaire's Mechanic
Burned Deep - Coming Soon

Writing As L.B. Gilbert
The Complete Elementals Saga
Discordia, A Free Elementals Story
Fire
Air
Water
Earth

A Shifter's Claim
Kin Selection
Eat You Up
Tooth and Nail
The When Witch and the Wolf

Charmed Legacy Cursed Angel Watchtowers
Forsaken

CREDITS

Cover Design: Robin Harper
http://www.wickedbydesigncovers.com

Editor: Cynthia Shepp
http://www.cynthiashepp.com/

Thank you to all of my readers especially to Jennifer Bergans for her editorial comments.

TAKE ME

A SINGULAR OBSESSION PREQUEL NOVELLA

TAKE ME
A SINGULAR OBSESSION NOVELLA

LUCY LEROUX

CHAPTER 1

"That's her," Jason White whispered, nudging his partner hard in the ribs.

Ethan grunted but didn't look up.

"C'mon, she's almost done with her order. You are finally here at the same time as she is, so look already before I kick you in the balls under this table."

Ethan rolled his eyes, but dutifully raised his head to check out the brunette standing at the coffee counter. He picked up his report again. "She's got nice legs. Can you please ask her out so we can get the hell back to the office? You know I don't like working up cases in public."

"Relax. No one can see the pics of the bodies from where we're sitting," Jason said.

They were investigating a fraud case with collateral damage in the form of two dead guys, but Jason wasn't overly concerned about privacy. Not in this empty corner of the cafe.

Jason and Ethan were both recent transplants to Boston. They had been assigned to FBI offices on opposite ends of the country but after working a few overlapping cases together, they decided they would enjoy being partners. Both wanted to move to a bigger city than the one they lived in. The bureau had recently seen fit to honor their transfer requests.

For the moment, they were stuck in the white-collar crime division, but to Jason's surprise, they were enjoying the work. The cases were more interesting than they'd initially supposed. Now if he could just get his love life on track, like his career...

"I can't walk up to a total stranger like that," Jason said, trying hard to appear as if he was studying the menu and not the girl. "She doesn't know me from Adam."

"You do it in bars all the time," Ethan said, eyes still on his report.

"That's different." Jason scowled, still staring at his Coffee Girl before hurriedly turning away when she swung around to glance at the cafe's other occupants. She turned back to the barista when the other woman said something to her.

"*Pathetic.*" Ethan laughed under his breath. "What is wrong with you? You act like you've never seen a pretty girl before."

"That woman at the counter is not *pretty*. She's beautiful," Jason corrected, stirring his coffee a little too hard.

It was true he was normally not this hesitant. A series of substandard dates and a few bad breakups had shot his confidence. His answer had been to avoid women for the past few months. That had been all right...for a while. Settling into a new city and a new department was time consuming. He figured he'd start dating in a few months. And then he'd seen *her*.

Coffee Girl was a goddess disguised as the girl next door. She was tall with long, dark hair that curled up at the ends. Whenever he saw her, she was wearing a fitted dress suit. She looked more like a cover model's version of a businesswoman than any executive in real life.

"You can't tell from here, but her eyes are green," Jason said. "And she's got a few freckles, but only on the bridge of her nose. It's as if someone designed her to check off all my boxes. She's freaking perfect."

Ethan sighed and looked over at Coffee Girl again. "Well, those tits are winners."

"Hey! That is the future Mrs. Jason White you're talking about. Watch your fucking mouth."

His partner smirked and glanced at the counter again. "Well, the barista sure seems to like her. And vice versa. She could be a lesbian."

Jason made a face. "No. I'm sure she's not. They're just friendly. She comes in here every day."

But now, he had doubts. It wasn't possible to tell nowadays. And the barista had just made her laugh. Coffee Girl had an amazing laugh. It was husky like she was coming down with a cold.

Maybe she is coming down with a cold. Whatever, he'd happily trade in some sick days if it meant he could lock lips with his dream girl.

The barista handed over Coffee Girl's order—one of those specialty drink monstrosities that was more whipped cream than coffee. She waved and laughed before walking out.

Ethan's head snapped up. "Seriously? You dragged me all the way out here, and you don't even talk to her?"

"It's not like we trekked miles on foot," Jason said. "We're two blocks from the office. And I brought you out here to check her out. That's all. And I'm not going to ask her out in front of you."

His partner gave him a disgusted look. "At this rate, you're not going to ask her out at all. You're going to camp out here all summer mooning over some random girl. Meanwhile, she's probably got a boyfriend or husband tucked away somewhere."

Jason's face fell, and his partner took pity on him. "Except I didn't see a ring," Ethan added.

"No, there's not one." Jason had made sure of that at least.

"But you have to do something soon. It's been like months, man."

Ethan was exaggerating. It had only been a couple of weeks since Jason had discovered this place. But his partner was right about one thing; he did need to figure out a way to talk to her. He was wasting time. If Coffee Girl didn't have someone in her life, she would soon enough. Women like that got snapped up quick and never stayed single long.

MAGGIE SHOULD HAVE BEEN WATCHING where she was going, but Liam had just sent a third text about the Bracebridge group arriving early. Consequently, she was looking down at her phone as she walked to the door of the cafe. That was why she missed the brick wall standing between her and the exit.

Except it wasn't a brick wall—it just felt like one. She'd run into someone, managing to upend her mocha all over her white dress shirt...her very hot mocha.

"Ah!" She dropped the cup and her coat, pulling her shirt away from her skin.

"Oh my god! I'm so sorry. Shit, let me help you." The man she'd walked into started patting her chest, trying to wipe off the hot coffee with his hands. His rapid brushing opened the buttons of her blouse, exposing her lacy brassiere and sticky décolletage, but he didn't appear to notice.

"Hey!" She looked up, ready to tell the bastard off, but she was instantly transfixed. The man with his hands on her breasts was *Coffee Guy*, the gorgeous blond from the cafe. Unbeknownst to him, he'd also had a starring role in some of her shower fantasies lately—and that was after only seeing him from a distance.

Up close, Coffee Guy was devastating, tall and broad shouldered with blond hair and sky-blue eyes. He had big hands too... She knew because they were still on her.

When she stared open-mouthed at him, he froze and glanced down at his hands. Flushing beet red, he straightened and snatched them away from her breasts.

"I wish you'd ordered a Frappuccino," he said before looking over her head. "Ice! Can we get some ice over here?"

Karen, the barista, hurried over with a cold towel. "Are you okay, Maggie?"

Maggie took it gratefully, wiping up coffee while simultaneously trying to cover herself with it. "I'm fine."

She had added extra cream, so the coffee hadn't been as hot as it normally was.

"Are you sure?" Coffee Guy asked, his blue eyes wide with concern. "Let me buy you a new coffee at least. And a shirt." What looked like panic filled his eyes, and his hands went to the buttons of his own dress shirt. He started to take it off.

Maggie laughed aloud and put out her hand. In a move she would regret later, she stopped him. "Really, I'm all right. I don't have time to wait for a new drink, but thank you anyway."

"Are you sure, Maggie? It'll just take a minute," Karen chimed in from behind her.

But her phone was ringing now, the Darth Vader theme she installed just for her older brother filling the air.

She turned back to the barista and gave her the towel, pulling the two halves of her shirt closed as best she could. It might have been missing a button now. Good thing her rooms were on the same floor as her office. "I have to run. Maybe next time. I think Liam will have kittens if I don't get back." Smiling at Coffee Guy, she ducked out the door before anything else could happen to her.

"At least let me pay for your dry cleaning," Coffee Guy said, following her outside the shop.

"I get mine done for free!" she called over her shoulder with a smile and a wave as the Notorious B.I.G.'s "Mo Money Mo Problems" began to play, signaling her other brother Patrick's call. The Bracebridge group organizer, an aggressive young woman named Rita, must be driving them batshit—most likely by trying to wheedle one of them into going out with her.

The pitfalls of being young and attractive almost-billionaires. Her brothers' timing couldn't have been worse, but they were counting on her. Maggie rescued her siblings from their determined admirers on a regular basis. Oh, well. *C'est la vie.* At least it was her life...

With one last laughing glance at Coffee Guy, she picked up her steps, her heels clicking on the pavement. He was still out on the sidewalk watching her when the Caislean's doorman Jonah opened the door for her.

CHAPTER 2

*E*than laughed his ass off when Jason told him what happened. Wiping tears from his eyes, Ethan thanked him. "God, I needed that after the Burns case. That's priceless. You're such an asshole."

Jason lips thinned. "Are you done yet?"

The out-of-breath chuckle that followed was answer enough. Five full minutes later, Ethan was ready to talk. "I can't believe you felt her up."

"It was an accident," Jason muttered.

He was typing out a report, hitting the keys hard enough to make his displeasure with his partner clear. Normally, he would have taken the time to shut Ethan up, but he was too distracted. Was Liam a boss or a boyfriend? What job had perks like free dry cleaning?

"At least you have a reason to talk to her again," Ethan observed. "Too bad it's going to be just to apologize."

"I'm still asking her out. I'm turning this sinking ship around." Or he would be if that Liam guy wasn't her husband or anything like that. "I know her name now and where she works—that big hotel across the street from the coffee shop."

"The new one with a weird name?"

"The Caislean. And it's not that new. Been there almost two years. A standard room goes for most of my paycheck."

Ethan hummed. "Are you sure she works there? Don't most of the staff there wear uniforms? I know I've seen some of them on the subway going home. They wear navy suits with little gold name tags."

Jason shrugged. "It's where she went in. Maybe she was cutting through their lobby to someplace else."

Ever the pessimist Ethan couldn't resist pointing out the obvious. "I bet they charge for that, too. That place is not the kind where they let you loiter. Could be she's a guest who will be leaving soon."

The sinking feeling in the pit of Jason's stomach was out of proportion to the facts at hand. He didn't even know Coffee Girl—Maggie—at all. So, he shouldn't be this downcast at the possibility she wasn't a Boston local.

His partner took pity on him. "Why don't we go and drop a wad on some overpriced whiskey at the hotel after work? They have a bar. I saw the entrance on the east side of the building. Too rich for my blood, but we can check it out tonight. Maybe you'll see her. And if you don't, you can go back to stalking her at the cafe."

"I'm not stalking her," he protested half-heartedly. "I drink coffee. They make a decent cup there..." Ethan grunted, and Jason side-eyed him. "What time?"

"Six."

The whiskey didn't cost twenty dollars. It was fourteen. Even though he still grumbled about the price, Ethan admitted it was pretty good. Jason paid for a few more, and they sipped, reclining in plush leather armchairs in the dark wood-paneled room.

"No wonder they charge so much for each room. This place must have cost a fortune to build," Ethan said, fingering the linen tablecloth on the table. He reached behind him to touch the paneling on the walls.

"Yeah, I don't think I've been to a bar set up like this. I feel like I'm in one of those private English clubs that Sherlock Holmes belonged to."

His partner snorted, leaned back in the rich leather, and took another sip.

Even though they had little chance of spotting Coffee Girl, Jason didn't mind coming out tonight. After closing a big case last week, he and Ethan had been rewarded with an even tougher one. They both needed to unwind, and this place was exactly what he needed.

Jason didn't like the sports bars Ethan inevitably chose for a post-work drink. They were too loud and the girls who came in were almost always taken—although it didn't seem to matter to Ethan. The guy usually left with a hot chick on his arm. Jason didn't have that kind of luck, despite what Ethan said. His partner thought he was too picky and maybe he was, but he was tired of settling.

Boston was a fresh start for his love life, and, this time, he was playing for keeps.

"The only thing missing from this place is a fine cigar," Jason observed, waving a waiter over to ask about the house whiskey. He wanted to buy his dad a bottle for Christmas, but he was disappointed. The spirit was a special blend specifically crafted for the hotel by an independent distiller in Scotland.

"We get asked that daily," the waiter said. "I'm afraid you can't buy it anywhere. The owners order a few cases for friends and family, but that's it. The hotel doesn't sell it by the bottle, although it may at some point. It's that popular."

"Hmm. Thanks anyway," Jason said, turning his attention to his partner when the other man shifted into his "alert" mode.

Ethan didn't sit up straighter or even move that much, but they had been partners long enough that Jason knew he'd spotted something. "Is it her?"

"Yes, and she's got a friend. A really *hot* friend."

Jason turned to see his curly-haired goddess with another tall brunette. The new one was a stunner too, possibly her sister. Both girls were dressed to party in short skirts and sparkly tops.

Those were not hotel uniforms.

"I guess you were right. She must be a guest." That was disappointing, but it was the kind of luck he was having with women lately. "Well, at least I can ask her for dinner before she leaves Boston."

"It's possible they work here and changed in the locker room to go clubbing. We should follow them. Maybe she won't spot you as the coffee attacker in a dark club."

Jason ignored him and stood up, prepared to go over to Maggie now so he could apologize. It was better to get it over with as soon as he could, especially if her time in town was limited. Before he could make it around the table, a man appeared out of nowhere. He was tall with closely cropped black hair, and he was wearing a suit that cost more than Jason's car.

The man beckoned the girls to him. Jason frowned when they greeted him warmly. Exchanging a glance with Ethan, Jason said, "I wonder if that is Liam?"

The waiter from his earlier query heard him, noting the direction of his gaze as he was wiping the table next to them. "Oh yeah, that's Liam all right. And if you're thinking what I think you're thinking, don't bother. Liam doesn't let anyone near his girls. Not unless you're a millionaire, and—" He broke off and checked out their clothes and shoes. "Sorry, I just don't think you have a shot."

With a little smirk, the guy went back to the bar. Jason watched as the mysterious Liam handed Maggie a piece of paper and leaned in to say something to her. She nodded and tucked it into her purse. The girls then turned and headed for the main doors with a wave.

Jason kept his eyes on the pair as Ethan came up behind him.

"So are we calling it?" his partner asked.

Jason turned to narrow his eyes with a hot glare. "Fuck no. Let's go after them."

Ethan laughed and shook his head. "Nothing brings out your competitive side like being told it can't be done."

"Don't spend this all in one place," Calen McLachlan said, handing over a handful of red-embossed VIP cards. "And don't forget to give Liam his."

Maggie beamed at her brother's best friend and took the cards. Calen was such a doll, a man completely at odds with his dangerous reputation.

Most people thought he was a criminal or worse. His father was an important figure in the Irish mob, but Calen wasn't a part of it. He'd been a surrogate brother for most of her life. Despite being nearly as overprotective as her two biological ones, Calen was, on occasion, capable of listening to reason.

Tonight was the one-month anniversary of his newest club opening. Siren had been a madhouse from opening day, and it was only now that Calen felt it had calmed enough for her to come and party with her friends. His VIP cards granted instant access to all his clubs and came with complimentary bottle service and other perks for an entire year. They were highly sought after.

"Does Peyton get one of these?" Her best friend should have been back from the bar but, knowing her, she had been waylaid by some random guy trying to attract her attention.

"Of course she does. In fact, she gets two so she can sell the other one to pay her rent like last year."

Maggie blinked. "You knew about that?"

One corner of Calen's lips lifted in a dry grin. "I did. Every card has a number. When one of those numbers turns up outside our circle, I know about it. If Liam isn't paying her enough, she can come work for me. I always need people with computer talent."

That would have been weird coming from a club owner, but Calen owned a string of them in addition to a slew of other investments, including shares in her family's hotels. As the event coordinator for the Caislean chain, she often worked with him and his staff when certain functions required an edgier vibe than the hotel could provide.

Organization and a fair amount of ruthless determination were the keys to Calen's success—not that she ever saw that side of him. She only heard about it.

"I don't think Liam will let her go," Maggie replied, aware of the irony of her words.

Her best friend was madly in love with her oldest brother. Peyton would have fought to stay at Liam's side, even if it meant running his errands and fetching his coffee. Luckily for everyone involved, her sometimes obtuse brother had recognized Peyton's tech skills and put her to work behind a computer ages ago.

Unfortunately for Peyton, Liam saw her as another little sister, one who needed to be smothered with overprotective acts at every turn.

Calen scowled. "Well, the next time her dad drinks away her paycheck, have Peyton check with me about some side work. A good programmer is worth their weight in gold."

Maggie raised her brows. She didn't know how Calen got his information, but it was always spot on. "You haven't told my brothers he fell off the wagon again, have you?"

"No, but I should. It wouldn't take much to get Donnie back into rehab. I wouldn't even need to get Liam involved, you know. One word from me and he'd go like a shot."

That was an understatement. Donnie, Peyton's dad, was scared shitless of Calen and her older brother Liam. They had made their opinion of him clear while in their teens—forcefully. He was afraid to cross them, but that didn't mean he didn't try to go around them.

Donnie mistakenly thought her other brother Patrick was a pushover, but he didn't know Trick would happily go backwoods on his ass if only Peyton would agree to it.

Maggie scratched her head, contemplating letting Calen intervene...but she couldn't encourage him. "I wish you would, but you know how she is about the douchebag. She wants to handle it on her own."

Calen's dark glance would have scared a lesser person. Maggie just gave him a purple-nurple.

"Hey!"

"I'm serious. I know that look on your face. Just leave it alone and let her deal with it. She's not stupid. Peyton will call in reinforcements if she needs them."

"*Fine*. Do you have the specs for the Chinese envoy's bash?"

"Right here," she said, whipping out the card her brother had given her earlier.

He studied the numbers and peppered her with questions about her plans until Peyton and her other girlfriends made it back to their private booth. One of them pestered him for an introduction to another VIP table full of men. One was a Russian cultural attaché named Mikael, who was currently staying at the hotel. After Calen had indulged her, he left to check on the manager.

Maggie had interacted with Mikael as part of her job. He made no secret of his interest, but she had a strict no-fraternization policy with the guests.

I may have to rethink that, she thought eyeing the handsome Russian. Between her overprotective brothers scaring off every man who approached her, and her busy schedule at the hotel, Maggie never got to meet eligible men. If she didn't have these regular girls' nights out, she would never leave the Caislean.

On that note, it was no doubt a bad idea to make this her regular nightspot. No doubt, Calen had his security staff keeping a close eye on them. But what made it a difficult place to meet men also made it a low-risk environment.

Maggie recognized that in many ways, she'd been sheltered and cosseted by the men in her life. However, it was hard to begrudge all that they did for her—not when their care overlapped her to her friends. Especially Peyton. In her opinion, her best friend needed someone like Calen or one her brothers in her corner. But that was another story...

Despite her early enthusiasm, as the night wore on, Maggie's opinion of Mikael the Russian nosedived. Like so many highfliers, Mikael had an overdeveloped sense of male privilege and entitlement, one that became more apparent the more he drank. She'd just removed his hand from her backside for the second time, surreptitiously waving away one of the VIP area's security guys.

Dancing with the girls was a much better way to rid herself of an unwanted suitor. Too many men found an outright challenge from another man a reason to pick a fight, and Mikael seemed like that type.

Unfortunately, her belief that she could shake him on the dance floor proved naïve. She had just given him a scathing set down that he likely didn't hear over the music when he put his hands on her ass for the third time. She pushed them off and spun on her heel to stalk away —and into the waiting arms of the gorgeous blond from this afternoon's disaster.

"Coffee Guy!"

Coffee Guy's grin was worthy of a toothpaste commercial. "I used to call you Coffee Girl. It's Maggie, right? My name is Jason—Jason White."

He looked over his shoulder, and the twinkle in his eye disappeared. As she watched, those baby blues grew ice cold as he eyed Mikael, who was stumbling behind her, his hands groping her backside as he caught up to them. Jason took her hand and guided her to his other side protectively so the other man couldn't touch her.

"Thank you for keeping Maggie company, but I'm here now so you can go," he said in a louder, much colder voice.

The Russian swore at him gutturally, reaching out to grab her wrist with a move she dodged. In one fluid move, Jason stepped in front of her.

"She's leaving with me," Mikael slurred.

Jason's answering smile left Maggie breathless. No man had ever looked more dangerous—not her brothers, not Calen. No one.

Oh, crap. This was precisely what she'd been hoping to avoid. Maggie put her hand on Jason's arm as the two men sized each other up. Mikael was taller with bulging muscles, and he had the added bravado that came with significant alcohol impairment.

But despite his adorable horn-rimmed glasses and slimmer stature, she instinctively sensed Jason was a greater threat. It was a flash of insight with no real evidence. To the outside observer, the Russian would be the obvious winner in a fight, but Maggie somehow knew with absolute certainty that Jason could and would destroy the larger man.

Except it didn't appear as if it would be a fair fight. Lining up behind the Russian were not one but two tough-looking bastards, Mikael's private security detail. They wouldn't be armed—Calen screened extensively for hidden weapons, but the heavy-set bruisers could do a lot of damage without weapons. On top of that, a crowd was gathering, forming a wall of flesh around them. She and Jason were effectively penned in with the irate Russian and his men.

Okay, being independent is one thing, being stupid is another.

Maggie started scanning the crowd for Siren's security men. She thought she saw one at the edge of the dance floor, but the crowd that surrounded them kept him from getting close. Blinking rapidly, she was trying to decide what to do when another man came up on their left. She recognized him; she'd seen him with Jason at the coffee shop. The newcomer whipped out a leather folio, flashed a badge at Mikael and the men behind him, and said something in Russian.

Maggie's grasp of the language was poor, but she still caught the words for "drug" and "search".

Michael sneered and drew his head back. His response used some of the more colorful Russian swear words she did know, but he backed off and left the dance floor. Disappointed, the crowd dispersed. Most went back to dancing without missing a beat.

"I could have handled that on my own," Jason told to the newcomer over the music.

"Two maybe, not three. Besides, having a partner means not going it alone." He turned to her. "Hi, I'm Ethan. Where's your friend?"

Maggie took in the bulging biceps and his cocky grin. This one was trouble. "Which friend?"

His grin was hot and flirtatious. "The other leggy brunette. Her hair is straighter than yours. Your sister, maybe?"

She shook her head. "Best friend, Peyton, and I don't see her. You'd have better luck with Shelley," she said, pointing out her other friend. Shelley, a sultry blonde, was talking to one of the club's regulars, Lisa, a woman who frequented the hotel.

Ethan took in Shelley's barely there red dress and wrinkled his nose. "I'm going to find Peyton."

She didn't want to tell him that even if he found her, his chances were next to nothing, so she let him go without further comment. Maybe the well-built officer would do the impossible—turn Peyton's head away from her brother.

When she looked back at him, Jason was watching her. Maggie bit her lip, hesitating, but she had a good feeling about him. Crooking her finger at him, she led him to a cozy booth in a darkened corner of the club away from all the dance floors.

"By partner, did Ethan mean you have a badge to match his...or is he your lover?" she teased as he sat next to her.

Jason laughed aloud—an excellent sign. Instead of answering, he took something out of his pocket and flipped it open for her. She squinted at the shiny gold badge. "The bureau has a satellite office a few blocks from the cafe. I've seen you there a few times and have actually been trying to figure out a way to say hello...so, hello."

Coming from any other man, she would have dismissed that line for the cheese it was, but coming from Coffee Guy, it sounded brilliant. Feeling drunk despite not having had a drop, she let Jason monopolize her for the next hour. When she realized how much time had passed, she was ready to go in search of her friends. At that moment, a waiter delivered a cocktail and a beer with a message written on a napkin.

I'm living vicariously through you, so don't even think about cutting this one loose. Enjoy the drinks. Calen paid. ;)
-Peyton

Giggling, Maggie put away the note. "Well, I guess my girls' night is a bust."

Jason grinned. "That's the best news I've heard all day—possibly all month."

His smile was infectious. "Well, I was lured out tonight with extravagant promises of having the best time by dancing until I dropped."

He stood and held out his hand. "Let me see what I can do."

THE NEXT DAY at the office, Jason found a strangely subdued Ethan.

"Guess who has a date tomorrow night?" Jason crowed as he sat down at his desk.

His partner's lips compressed. "I take it all went well after I left?"

Jason leaned back into his office chair with a grin. "It did indeed—at least by my definition. Since the night didn't end in my bed, it would be a fail by yours. But I'm happy."

Ethan's expression darkened, and Jason frowned. "Hey, what's wrong? I thought you'd be pleased I finally got off my ass and got the girl—without humiliating myself in the process."

Ethan ran a hand through his dark hair. "Don't get me wrong. I am glad you finally made progress. Maggie's a looker. So are her friends, especially the one who wouldn't give me the time of day...but didn't you notice the vibe at the club?"

"You mean the guy hassling her? The Russian? Of course I noticed him. But he didn't bother us after that scene on the dance floor. I made sure she got home safe without any interference. Put her in a cab at two myself. Did you turn up something on him?"

His partner nodded. "As a matter of fact, I did, under the name Dolohov, which I got from the bartender. But the stuff was small time —a little innuendo from Interpol. Nothing solid."

"Then what's wrong?" Ethan wouldn't be making an issue of this without a reason. He wasn't the type to yell smoke without a fire.

Jason's brow rose as Ethan sat up and looked around, checking to make sure none of the other agents were close enough to overhear him.

"Well, I was trying to get Maggie's friend to dance. She was shooting me down. Not a big deal. I don't push when the lady isn't interested—although I admit it doesn't happen all that often. But in this case, it was pretty fucking revealing."

"How so?"

"The security staff. I noticed them clocking us after the thing with the Russian, which was normal. But they kept tabs on both of us for the rest of the night."

"Good security should do that," Jason pointed out.

"Yeah, but they generally don't. However, last night they kept multiple guys on us. I don't blame you for not noticing, you were busy, but they made themselves visible when that Peyton girl shot me down. It was like they were getting ready to jump me. The only reason they didn't is because the girl signaled them to stand down. The whole thing was kind of fishy if you ask me—especially when I found out who owns that club."

"I'm not going to like this, am I?"

"I doubt it," Ethan said. "Do you remember that rundown we got on all the local organized crime syndicates when we first transferred?

One of the major players was a guy called Colman McLachlan, Irish mob. His son, Calen, owns Siren. This is his picture."

Ethan turned his monitor toward him. The photo was of a fit dark-haired man in his late twenties. Jason recognized him from the club. It was the guy who'd handed Maggie something—the one who had kissed her cheek and hugged her before taking off for parts unknown.

"Knowing someone shady doesn't mean anything. Maggie is a good-looking girl who hangs with others of her kind. Clubs give preferential treatment to hot women—especially when they travel in packs. Their presence encourages men to come in and drop wads of cash at the bar," Jason said aloud, mulling it over.

He suspected his partner was trying not to roll his eyes when he asked, "So you saw this Calen guy all over her too?"

Jason threw a pencil at him. "It was barely a kiss, and it was on the cheek."

"Still kind of chummy considering who he is." Ethan picked up the pencil and twirled it. "If I were you, I'd keep an eye on the situation."

"Fine," Jason grumbled. "But I bet I'm right. I'm sure Maggie has no idea who this McLachlan character really is, let alone who his people are."

CHAPTER 3

There was a picture of the mobster's son on her phone. *And he had his arm around her.*

Although the pic only showed them from the waist up, he could see that Maggie was wearing a bikini on what was clearly some far-off beach. Behind her and the grinning asshole with the oversized pecs was an expanse of sugar-white sand. In the distance was an impossibly blue ocean, the kind one had to fly to the Caribbean to find.

Fuck!

It was their seventh date, and Jason had convinced himself that Maggie was as close to perfect as human women got. She didn't insist on being taken to two-hundred-dollar dinners or drinks every night. Unlike the last few girls he dated, Maggie liked eating fast food—if it was tasty and hot, she was happy. She didn't count calories or make him feel guilty by eating only rabbit food in front of him. Instead, she stayed active.

Maggie was always on the go. Somehow after running all over town for work, she still had the energy to join him for a raucous night of ice skating that got unexpectedly competitive.

It was the first time I've been asked to leave a skating rink.

Maggie was hot and sweet with just enough wildness to keep him on his toes. After only a few weeks, he knew that he was falling for her—hard.

But then she'd made the mistake of leaving her phone out in the open after eating an entire plateful of wings. Before he could stop himself, he'd snatched the thing up, easily deciphering the passcode by trying the numbers that had traces of barbecue sauce on them. Among the many pictures of the Caislean hotel, he found some of her girlfriends and a small, but significant, amount of the mobster.

To make matters worse, Calen McLachlan wasn't the only young and attractive man in her pictures either. There was a whole assortment to curse over. Prominent among them were two other dark-haired men who looked like brothers. Those two were way too liberal with their hugs in the photos.

Out of the corner of his eye, he saw Maggie emerging from the restaurant bathroom. He quickly put the phone back on top of her purse. Forcing a smile, he tried to pick up their conversation where they had left off, reminding himself to take a serious look at McLachlan. If he saw something to alarm him, he would confront her about him. Until then, he would leave it alone.

Everyone was entitled to a past, right?

I'M FALLING IN LOVE. Maggie had never felt this way about a man before. Ever since that first night at the club, Jason had been constantly in her thoughts or at her side.

He hadn't played any games—no waiting three days to call for him. He had wanted to see her again as soon as possible, so they met during their lunch hour. Lunch had led to dinner and phone calls that lasted until two in the morning every night that week. The only reason the conversations didn't continue until dawn was because they both worked.

Of course, not everything was perfect. She was too anxious to tell him her real circumstances. Things were going well now, but Jason

LUCY LEROUX

might balk or freak out when he found out her family owned the Caislean.

It had happened before. She had dated a nice guy named Maleek who had a regular office job. When he found out who she was, he'd become irate, breaking up with her on the spot. He accused her of being just another rich girl, a parasite who didn't have to work for a living but lived off her inheritance.

Maggie had tried to defend herself—she and her brothers had built their hotel business almost from scratch. Right after her parents had died, there had been some trying financial times. Liam's drive and ruthless determination had changed all that. He had harnessed their other brother Patrick's charm and wit and turned him into a killer salesman, one capable of meeting Liam's exacting standards. Together, they had built an empire.

Although they had accomplished a lot without her, Maggie had rolled up her sleeves and done her part as soon as she was old enough. But that didn't stop people from labeling her as just another rich socialite, despite her intentionally low public profile.

It was with some apprehension that she'd finally told Jason her last name at the end of their first date. If he had a problem with her wealth, she wanted to know sooner rather than later. But Jason had just smiled and asked her for a second date with an excited, "Do you like ice skating?"

She'd said yes, and things had taken off from there. Because Jason was new to the city, he was eager to see and do everything. It was fun acting as an unofficial tour guide. He wasn't backward about telling her what he didn't enjoy either—which was nice. As a hotel heiress, she had attracted a few yes-men before, and it was annoying when they pretended to love everything she did. Jason hated hockey and Indian food, both of which she adored. Aside from that, and an aversion to certain bars, he was more than willing to run all over Boston with her.

Unlike so many men, Jason never assumed she would only enjoy typical date activities like dinner and dancing. When it was his turn to suggest an activity, he took her go-kart racing and to an arcade. Maggie knew he was something special when she kicked his butt on a vintage *Street Fighter* game. Instead of grumbling or asking for a rematch, he cheered with good humor. Her heart gave a hard squeeze when he held her hand up like a boxing announcer before declaring her the winner to the entire arcade. His joy was genuine, with no trace of macho resentment.

A guy who let you win was one thing, but one who took pride in your victory was quite another. Her FBI agent was fun and easygoing, but there was something about him. He made her feel secure and like she was flirting with danger at the same time.

Christmas was only a few weeks away. Although there was no snow on the ground, the city was decorated in gilt and cheery reds. This was her favorite time of the year, and she and Jason had been on another amazing date. They'd gone to her favorite sushi place in Chinatown and were cutting through Boston Common to a bar she knew served mulled wine.

In no real hurry to get out of the cold as long as Jason was with her, Maggie chatted to him about her day. She kept her references vague enough so he didn't pick up on exactly what she did. As far as Jason knew, she was a social coordinator for the hotel. It wasn't a real position, but she would have to think about adding it to her official job title. It encapsulated what she did rather well.

Both were so engrossed in their conversation that they didn't notice the pair of thieves sizing them up—not until one of them ran past, hitting Jason hard from the left.

"Hey!" Jason yelled, turning to chase after the guy. As he did, the second man came up on her right. After snatching her purse, the second thief ran in the opposite direction. Unfortunately for her, he didn't notice the purse was slung around her shoulder. It got caught on her neck, choking her as the man made a break for it.

The assailant kept pulling until they were in a violent tug-of-war she would almost assuredly lose. Desperate to breathe, Maggie tried to pull the strap over her head. She no longer cared if the asshole got her purse—she needed air.

But the thief simply yanked it back, unaware the strap was still around her neck. Coughing and gasping, she pulled back on the strap, her eyes watering as she struggled to breathe—and scream.

A loud roar filled her ears. For a moment, she thought it was the wind. Belatedly, she realized it was Jason. His howl of outrage was deafening. Before she could blink, his hand shot out in front of her face, pulling on the strap with enough force to make the second thief lose his footing. The man spun and fell toward them, his face on a collision course with Jason's fist.

Maggie could feel the thud in her bones when the two made contact. The thief fell to the ground and didn't get up.

Jason put his foot on the fallen man's back and kept yelling, "Hands up!" It took her a moment to realize he was shouting at the other man, the one who had hit him. The first man had only made it a few yards before realizing one of his intended victims was pointing a gun at him. By the time her gaze swung back, the second thief had his hands up, pleading with Jason not to shoot.

The rest was a blur. Running feet signaled the approach of a pair of cops in uniform.

"Stop right there," the first uniform bellowed, his gun out.

"I'm reaching for my badge," Jason said as he reached into his coat and flipped open the leather folio that held his identification. "These men tried to mug us. I want you to take them in."

The second officer put his gun away and reached for his handcuffs. Before she knew it, the two thieves were arrested in short order.

Still in a daze, Maggie marveled as Jason managed to wrap up everything succinctly. He had an innate authority the other cops deferred to without question. Throughout his discussion with them, he kept an arm around her, caressing her back with a comforting, and most likely unconscious, touch.

"This is my office number," Jason said. "I want you to call me after you file the charges. Make sure to dot your I's and cross your T's. I don't want these shits getting off on a technicality. Wherever these guys go after—I want to know."

Maggie rubbed her neck and shuddered, still too stunned to say very much. Once the cops took the men away, she tried to speak, despite her painful throat. Her voice was hoarse and thready, a detail that made Jason curse aloud. He wiped the involuntary tears she hadn't been aware she was shedding.

"Those assholes are lucky I didn't see these tears before they got hauled away." He kissed the tracks on her cheeks. "Baby, I should take you home."

To her, home was the hotel. With both Liam and Patrick in town, there was no way they would leave her alone if she brought a man to her rooms. In fact, once they found out about the attempted mugging, they would insist on having her examined by the on-site physician. The news of the attack would spread like wildfire after that. In no time, they would be inundated with concerned staff—her extended family.

She could picture the chaotic scene now. "I have sort of a roommate situation," she rasped. "Can you take me to your house?"

Jason's lips parted and his eyes heated like quicksilver. After a beat, he nodded. "Yeah, I can do that."

THE BRIGHT OVERHEAD lights revealed the friction burn on Maggie's neck in stark detail. Jason muttered under his breath as he gently lifted her curls out of the way and tilted her head toward the light to better illuminate the injury.

She was sitting on his bathroom counter next to the sink, her legs hanging off the side in front of him as he conducted a thorough examination.

"Really, I'm fine now," she repeated for the second time.

She was cupping the mug of warm grog he'd thrown together when they arrived at his apartment. It was his grandmother's recipe for colds, but it worked as a throat tonic as well. The fact it was made with liberal amounts of whiskey and honey had done a lot to smooth Maggie's frayed nerves. At least her hands had stopped shaking.

Her voice did sound much better, but Maggie still winced every time she swallowed—which she did again at that moment.

Jason swore. He was an FBI agent for fuck's sake. Maggie should have been safe with him, not a hair on her head touched. The raw red mark on her delicate skin was a personal affront, a visible indictment on his ability to protect her.

"Could you stop looking like that?" she asked in a low voice.

He frowned. "Like what?"

"Like you want to punch through the wall. I'm okay, really, thanks to you and this wicked brew." She held up the mug and grinned before taking another sip.

He set the mug aside and pressed his forehead to hers. "I promise from now on, I will take better care of you."

She pressed her lips to his for a too-brief moment. "That's very sweet, but I'm not mugged on a regular basis."

"Neither am I." He sighed. "In fact, it's a first for me. Ethan will never let me live this down. We're trained to be aware of our surroundings." He paused to frown at her. "I was too focused on our conversation…and the way your lips move. You're an incredible distraction."

Maggie's eyes widened in mock outrage. "So, this is my fault?"

Feeling some of his levity returning, he grinned. "Completely."

She giggled and tried to kick him. Her foot glanced off his leg and slid up until it was pressed to the outside of his thigh. Heat pulsed through him, and he stared down at her face. He was strangely out of breath. He stepped closer, tugging her other legs until they were both wrapped around his waist.

His hands moved to cup her ass, pulling her tight against him. His self-control, already threadbare after the mugging, went up in flames the moment her arms went up around his neck. He took possession of her mouth, his lips slanting over hers as their tongues met and tangled.

As he pressed closer to her, his cock throbbed behind the thick denim of his jeans. She moaned. Impatient to have her underneath him, he swung her into his arms and carried her to the nearest place he could lay her down. He set Maggie on the overstuffed micro-suede cushions of his couch, stretching on top of her when she tugged at his shirt.

Heat flooded him, and his shaft swelled rigid. Aware that he was close to bursting, he tried to slow things down. The kisses lengthened and stretched, growing languorous, but still deliciously hot. His mouth flamed up her neck and broke off, suddenly recalling her injury. Was he hurting her?

"What's wrong?" Maggie's voice was still hoarse.

He swore under his breath before sitting up, away from her. "Shit. Okay, I really want you to stay, but not because of what happened tonight. I'm sorry. I'm not feeling very levelheaded here. I'm still pissed I let you get hurt."

Maggie sat up too, blushing a rosy pink. "That wasn't your fault. You have to stop blaming yourself. It was a random mugging. Because of you, those guys are in jail...but maybe you're right. I should head home. I'm not feeling very steady myself."

He took a deep breath and exhaled slowly. "Why don't I call you a cab? Tomorrow, we can meet at the cafe for lunch."

"I will call one, but lunch sounds good," she said before looking around bashfully as if she were suddenly self-conscious. "I should get going."

He waited until the car was five minutes out before walking her to the door. "Text me when you arrive home," he requested.

She nodded and kissed him one more time as he opened the door. It closed after her with a loud click.

Fuck!

Jason knew he'd done the right thing, but it was literally killing him. So far, he'd managed to stay a gentleman on their dates. Too many times, his relationships had spiraled after getting physical too soon. His gut told him Maggie was special, and he was determined to do this right. Even though it hurt, he kept a tight rein on his urges and impulses around her, limiting their contact to a few brief kisses. He was determined to take things slow. However, after tonight, his resolve was in tatters.

At least I'm not the only one having a hard time in the restraint department. Maggie had been right there with him on the couch, at least until he'd done the selfless thing and sent her home. *Idiot...*

He heard a small noise. Jason put his eye to the peephole. She hadn't left. As he watched, she raised a hand as if to knock, but hesitated, undecided.

Please stay.

Disappointment flooded him when she put her hand down and

turned away. He slumped against the door. Raising his head, he stepped away, walking to the bathroom for another cold shower. At least he was saving a lot on his heating bill this month.

He spun around at the sound of the knock. Lunging for the door, he threw open the door and pulled Maggie into his arms.

CHAPTER 4

The door had barely closed at her back when Jason had her pinned against it.

"Oh, thank god," he breathed into her mouth before kissing her so ravenously her vision swamped out.

Whimpering, Maggie could feel her bones melting as his mouth took possession, pouring all his heat and frustration into her. His hands moved over her, tugging at her clothes. His quick fingers opened her shirt, pulling it apart so his mouth could reach her décolletage. Jason ran his tongue over the top of her breasts, pressing her closer with a hand against her back like he was trying to prevent her from escaping—as if she wanted to.

His mouth closed over one lace-covered nipple and sucked hard, sending a shooting sensation straight to her cunt. Her channel spasmed hungrily, and she gasped and moaned aloud. The sound appeared to drive him crazy. Already impatient, Jason's hands tore at the waistband of her wool pants, tugging them down and off, along with her panties, in one motion.

He started to pull her away from the door, but she was too impatient. "Here! *Now*," she panted.

This time when she wrapped her legs around him, she was naked from the waist down. His muscular arms held her to him, her back to the door as his cock pressed against her. The silky head stroked her wet pussy, parting her inner folds with a blunt, insistent pressure.

"Christ, you are so tight," he said in her ear before sucking the lobe into his mouth as he slowly and inexorably pushed inside her.

A tremor ran through her, and she tightened her hold on him. "It's been a long time," she whispered back evasively, worried he would stop if he knew the truth. She couldn't let him—her whole body was crying out for him, aching for his possession. Jason was too honorable for his own good. If he knew she was a virgin, he'd stall and want to talk it out to make sure she was certain of him.

This had to happen *now*; she couldn't wait anymore.

Time slowed as Jason flexed his hips, driving his cock inside her to the very hilt. Maggie cried out, feeling impossibly full, the hypersensitive nerve endings in her passage firing all at once as they were overwhelmed by pain and pleasure. It was too much—he was too big and there was too much sensation in a place that had never experienced anything remotely like this before.

Jason withdrew and stroked back in. The pain receded into the background as a wave of pleasure rolled through her core. It tightened and pulled around him involuntarily.

Maggie was suddenly angry. Why hadn't anyone told her it could be this way? *What the hell had she been waiting for all this time?*

Desperate for more contact, she dug her nails into his shoulders, burying her face in his neck. She breathed deeply, drawing his scent into her lungs in an effort to wrap herself up in him. *Him. Jason. You were waiting for him*, she reminded herself.

Any sense of pride and self-composure she might have possessed was lost—dust in a blaze of hormones and long-denied sexual gratification. She clung to him and sobbed. "More. Please God, more," she begged.

Jason's answering laugh sounded desperate, like he was in pain as well. He didn't answer—didn't waste a breath on words. Instead, his grip on her ass tightened and he drove harder, thrusting faster and faster. Pinned, she held on blindly, her focus—all sensation—trained on his hard, velvety staff as it slipped in and out, rocking her against the door with each thrust.

Like the work of some mad alchemist, the friction and tug of him transmuted into ecstasy. She contracted and fluttered around him, squeezing and clutching him with all her strength. Jason growled, one hand moving behind her head to protect her before he sank deep, slamming her into the door and grinding against her. His cock swelled and jerked, his hot seed jetting and flooding her with warmth.

Panting, Jason adjusted his grip, letting them both slide down the door until they collapsed on the floor.

He caught his breath and raised his head to kiss her softly. "Are you all right? You are so small. I didn't hurt you, did I?"

He was still inside her, soft now. She adjusted her legs, keeping them wrapped around him. "I'm good—incredible actually. But I don't think I can move."

Her entire body felt weak. Now she knew what people meant by completely spent. It was doubtful she could raise her arms higher than her head.

Jason moved slightly, kissing her forehead as he left her body. "That's not going to be a problem," he promised before picking her up and carrying her to his bedroom.

CHAPTER 5

Maggie cursed Jason's beautiful body as she ran down the narrow stairs that led to the Caislean's employee entrance in the basement.

She had been determined to leave his place before dawn. If she managed to reach the hotel early enough, she could rush to her rooms before her brothers came around to pick her up for brunch.

It was a family tradition from back in the days of her parent's bed and breakfast. They always ate brunch in the main dining room every Sunday afternoon. She had expected the tradition to die when her parents did, but Liam made sure it didn't. No matter how busy or bad things got in those difficult years after their deaths, Liam made sure they always reserved that time for each other—even if brunch was restricted to juice and cereal because they couldn't afford more at the time.

How many times had she heard, *'Omelets and waffles are for the guests'*?

These days, brunch was an extravagant affair, courtesy of the hotel's French chef. More often than not, it was just her and Peyton because her brothers traveled so much for work. But if they were in town, brunch as a family—plus Peyton—was a given.

By the time she managed to drag herself from Jason's warm bed, it was late afternoon and brunch was long over. Peyton had promised to cover for her, but her best friend had never been able to lie to Liam. Even as a child, Peyton had sung like a bird whenever her older brother had questioned them about their little childhood transgressions. It was her only flaw.

Jason hadn't understood why Maggie needed to get back to the hotel. After making love two more times that morning, he had pulled out all the stops to convince her to stay with him. His arsenal was impressive—there was that delectable six-pack and those lickable biceps...

Damn, she was too warm now.

I have to tell him I live here, she thought, furtively ducking inside the service elevator and taking it to the main lobby. At this hour, she should be all right. The staff took staggered lunch breaks, but the majority should have finished at least half an hour ago. If she hurried, there was a better-than-decent chance at getting to the penthouse elevators unimpeded. If anyone did see her, they would hopefully believe she'd been out running errands and wouldn't notice she was wearing the same outfit from the night before...

Maggie breathed a huge sigh of relief when she unlocked the door to her suite without running into anyone.

"*Where have you been?*"

She screamed and dropped her purse on the floor.

"For fuck's sake, Liam. Don't sneak up on me like that!" She bent to pick up her purse. "You damn near gave me a heart attack."

"Who is sneaking?" He threw up his hands before pointing at her. "And don't swear. It's not ladylike."

Despite the fact it was Sunday, Liam was dressed in a navy-blue suit and tie. Behind him, Patrick was sitting on her plush silk damask couch. Unlike Liam, Trick was more casually dressed in slacks and button-down shirt with the sleeves rolled up—and he was smirking.

"You may bite my lady butt," she said, regressing a few years and rolling her eyes at their older brother.

Trick snorted. "But you have someone for that now...or am I wrong? Are we not witnessing your very first walk of shame?"

Maggie drew herself up to her full height. It was, unfortunately, half a foot shorter than either of her brothers. "I have nothing to be ashamed about. I am a grown woman who spent the night with her significant other—the way grown-ups sometimes do. If either of you has a problem with that you can...you can..."

She trailed off, trying to think of a threat dire enough for her brothers to take seriously.

Liam put his head on his hands like he was getting a migraine. "No, this isn't happening. I'm not ready."

Trick threw him a sympathetic glance, but he was more philosophical. "Liam, she's over twenty-one. She's overdue for a real relationship—and it could be worse. It could have been one of the skeevy Europeans who are always hitting on her when they stay here. Or worse, that Neanderthal Russian Mikhael. This Jason guy is an FBI agent."

Maggie's mouth dropped open. "How did you know that?" She narrowed her eyes at Liam. "You made Peyton spill, didn't you?"

"No, so you can relax. I did try, but your BFF's lips were sealed on this matter." Liam looked annoyed that his usual powers of persuasion had failed. "Calen is the one who told me about your new boyfriend's job."

"Calen did?" Who told him?

"What did you expect with the man and his partner flashing their badges at Siren? Calen's security can tell a fake one from a real one," Liam added with a growl.

Maggie sighed and threw herself on the couch next to Trick. "There's no need for the third degree. Jason is a good guy," she said before sitting up straighter. "No, I take it back. Jason is a good man. He's had two serious girlfriends and is tired of dating around. Plus, he calls his mom every Monday. Earlier this year, he refinanced her house when she almost lost it. He makes every other payment to help her out, which is why his own apartment is so tiny. And you know what they say about men and the way they treat their mothers..."

Liam wasn't impressed. He frowned. "And does this good man know how much you are worth yet?"

She opened her mouth to give him a snappy answer, but then she remembered and hesitated.

"*I knew it.*"

Liam's dour expression was becoming way too familiar. Maggie couldn't remember the last time he had smiled.

"Stop making that face or it will stick that way. I'm going to take a shower," she said, standing up and heading to her bathroom before they noticed the mark on her neck. Knowing Liam, he'd assumed Jason had done it. "And our money won't be an issue. Not to Jason."

Her older brother couldn't resist having the last word. "I hope you're right. We don't need a repeat of the Maleek incident."

CHAPTER 6

*J*ason walked into his office wearing his now-habitual grin. There was one plastered on his face most days now, thanks to Maggie. They had been dating for almost two months—not that he was counting anymore. He'd decided after week one that she was the girl he was going to marry.

He settled in at his desk with a cup of coffee, tackling the long list of emails that had accumulated over the weekend. Ethan walked in a bit later, looking haggard.

"Let me guess...she was a stewardess?" Jason didn't bother to duck the crumpled notepaper that came flying at his head. He started on the next email. "Okay then, a pharmaceutical rep? They only let the hottest of the hot do that these days, right?"

"That's not it."

"So what does she do?" Jason asked distractedly.

Despite his best effort, his inbox never got any smaller. *They never mention how much paperwork there is during recruitment.* He raised his head to find Ethan staring at him.

"I wasn't with a woman last night. I met up with a local detective. Do you remember the background check we ran on the younger McLachlan?"

"Yeah, we didn't find anything concrete. Calen McLachlan has never been convicted of anything. He's never even been a person of interest."

"I know, but our search triggered one of the local's alert. There's this detective with BPD, name of Dawson. It seems he's been running surveillance on Calen McLachlan for months now."

Fuck. Why did his love life always have to get so complicated?

"Why didn't it come up in our search?" he asked.

"It's off the books. Dawson used to be part of the joint organized crime task force back in the day, but those guys stopped running Calen McLachlan a while ago. There was officially no reason to keep it up. Dawson was against ending the investigation, but the BPD brass shut him down."

"Then what the hell kind of evidence does this guy have to twist your panties in a bunch?"

His partner glared at him, but Jason just waved at him to get on with it.

"Well, the way Dawson puts it, McLachlan keeps a rabid team of lawyers on retainer and BPD resources are tight. Dawson claims the higher-ups don't want to deal with the hassle of getting sued, so they've nixed getting a team inside Siren every time he's requested one. Same for all of McLachlan's other businesses."

Jason frowned. "Sounds like Dawson has a fat lot of nothing."

"Could be," Ethan acknowledged. "But I think you need to look at all the photos he has."

"Why?"

His partner leaned in confidentially. "Because your girl is all over them."

Jason held up a hand. "So they know each other. We knew that already." *And that they possibly dated.*

"Shit, I didn't want to be the one to say it, but you need to talk to this guy. Look at his surveillance, listen to his story, and then make your own decision. If Maggie is the angel you think she is, the guy's spiel won't hold water. But if there's something there, you need to know now. Before you get any deeper." Ethan leaned back and squinted at him. "Although I suspect it's already too late, isn't it? You're already in love with her."

Jason didn't bother answering.

CHAPTER 7

Maggie batted the hand away and rolled over in bed. "Five more minutes," she muttered.

She felt someone sitting on the side of the mattress, making her body shift toward the weight. Grunting, she grabbed the pillow and put it over her head. "What time is it?" she asked, her voice muffled.

"Seven."

Pushing the pillow out of the way, she squinted at Jason. "Why in God's name are you waking me at seven AM on a weekend?"

She thought he winced. It was hard to tell with the way her eyes were refusing to focus. "I'm sorry, but I have to go to work."

Maggie rolled closer with effort. She had never been a morning person.

"On *Sunday*?" She guessed that meant brunch was out.

Maggie had finally decided to take Jason to the Caislean to introduce him to her brothers. She was going to casually mention that they wanted to meet him, and if he agreed to go today, she would spill her guts about their role at the hotel.

Technically, only Trick wanted Jason to come for brunch. Liam didn't want to meet him at all. Every time Trick brought it up, their oldest brother would shake his head and start muttering that he "wasn't ready".

But she *was* ready. Keeping the full truth of who she was had started to feel dishonest. Technically, she hadn't lied to Jason. She had told him her name and where she worked. It was just that he hadn't put two and two together and connected her to the Tylers who owned the hotel—if he knew who that was. Aside from the Hiltons and the Marriots, how many people could actually name a hotel owner? Especially when they didn't plaster their name on the side of the building?

How did one tell a boyfriend they made more in a year than he would ever earn in a lifetime?

To confuse matters more, Jason had been acting distant the last few days. He'd been so distracted at the movies last night that he was unable to repeat a single plot point afterward. Together with Peyton, she had dissected everything he'd said to her, trying to figure out if he was withdrawing because he wanted to end things.

However, Jason continued to say and do all the right things, and he'd certainly been eager for her to spend the night.

"I'm not going to the office," he answered after a slight hesitation. "I'm meeting up with a local detective about something. It's important."

That sounded serious enough. "Oh, okay. I'll get up," she said, sitting up and trying to hide a yawn.

"Don't be silly." He smiled softly, his blue eyes warming as they took in her sleepy face. "You should stay. I expect this meeting to be over soon. In fact, I'm not sure why I'm going because I'm pretty sure this guy is blowing smoke up my ass. But I promised my partner I would give him a hearing. Why don't you sleep in? I'll be back before you wake up again."

Staying in his place while he was gone had to be some sort of relationship milestone. *Vogue* or *Elle* could have told her which one if she read those types of magazines. "Are you sure? Wouldn't you rather meet up later...maybe for brunch?"

"I'm almost positive I'll be back long before that. Stay. Sleep." He grinned down at her, ratcheting her body temperature up by several degrees. "I'll enjoy waking you up again."

Maggie snorted and put her head back down on the mattress. "Hurry back then."

Jason passed a hand down the exposed skin of her hip, stroking her softly before walking to the door. "I will."

BY QUARTER TO NOON, Maggie was starving. She had showered and dressed thirty minutes earlier in the wrinkle-free wrap dress she'd stuffed in her purse. Jason had given her a spare toothbrush the first time she'd spent the night, but dressing in the same clothes as the night before was not an experience she cared to repeat.

The little things you learn in your first relationship...

After deciding she was too hungry to wait for Jason's meeting to be over, she grabbed her things. Phone in hand, she was in the building's lobby texting her brothers and Peyton, telling them she was on her way for brunch and to save her some pancakes. She didn't bother to mention that Jason wasn't coming with her because she hadn't told her brothers he might. Peyton was the only one in her confidence, and since Maggie had chickened out for two Sundays in a row, her friend wouldn't be surprised when she appeared alone.

She was about to hit send when she saw her man coming through the glass doors of the main entrance. "Hey! You're just in time to join me for brunch at the hotel."

"What's wrong?"

Jason looked pale and clammy. His face was damp and slightly green, as if he was coming down with something. She stopped in front of him with a frown before putting her hand on his forehead. "Are you all right? You look ill."

Would chicken soup work for whatever this was? The hotel's chef made a delicious one. Maybe she could have someone run a tub of it over to him.

Jason looked down at her, his face more intent than the time they'd gone to play laser tag. He put his hands on her shoulders. "Maggie, I want you to listen to me. I really care about you—"

Her heart sped up. "I care about you, too."

He nodded abruptly. "That's great. I'm so glad, but I need to say this all at once or—I don't care what you've done before you met me. All I care about is where we go from here." He leaned in and lowered his voice to a whisper. "If after you hear what Dawson has to say, you decide not to help or you feel like you're in danger, I can help you. I *will* help you. We… we could even leave. We can get out of this town and not come back."

Maggie's head drew back. "Okay, you are definitely sick with something because none of that made sense. And who is Dawson?"

"I'm Dawson."

Maggie peeked around Jason. His partner Ethan was standing there with a second man.

The stranger was only a few years older than Ethan and Jason, but he appeared worse for wear. Although his clothing was clean, it managed to look shiny and unkempt, as if it had a layer of something greasy over it. Along with the thin, tan-colored hair and paunch, he had an air of dishevelment one usually had to work at to achieve.

She did not like the way he was looking at her.

"*Who* is this?" she asked Jason, but his hands were covering his face. Ethan was no help either. When her questioning glance fell on him, he inhaled deeply and put his hands on his hips. She couldn't tell what he was thinking behind the reflective mirror sunglasses he was wearing. *Just like the FBI agents on TV.*

"You're in a whole world of trouble, little girl," Dawson said, stepping up to lean over her intimidatingly. "You and your boyfriend Calen McLachlan. But I'm here to get you out of it."

He smiled as if he were doing her a favor.

Was this some sort of joke? "Wait, you think Calen is my *what*?"

Maggie's eyes widened as she pointed at Jason. "*That* is my boyfriend. And what the hell are you talking about? I haven't done anything wrong."

"Not sure that one is gonna be your boyfriend after this." Dawson smirked, tilting his head at Jason.

"*Hey*. You agreed to be civil," Jason snapped. He turned to Maggie, his eyes a stormy grey. "Maggie, can you please come upstairs? We need to talk."

He reached out for her, but she backed away with her hands up. "I don't know what this is all about, but you are making a mistake. I know Calen, but we've never been a thing. He's like a brother."

Dawson clicked his tongue at her. "Sure he is, kid. Listen, I've heard them all. I know all about you and your *friend*," he said, putting air quotes around the last word. "Out of courtesy to another branch of law enforcement, I agreed to do this on the down-low. But if you want to do this the hard way, we can go to the station and do this on the books. Your choice."

The man's obnoxious swagger permeated every word.

"You are all either criminally insane or too stupid to live." She turned to the two men she knew and waved at Dawson. "And why does this one talk like he's in some sort of fifties police drama? Is he for real?"

Ethan snickered, but Jason closed his eyes and squeezed them shut tight.

She was contemplating going forward with her punch-the-sneer-off-Dawson's-face plan. *The hotel has excellent lawyers. I can get away with it.*

"So, what's it going to be? Upstairs or downtown?"

Her mind rebelled at the thought of having any sort of conversation with this cretin in her lover's apartment.

Ex-lover. Maggie narrowed her eyes at Jason, hoping her contempt was coming across loud and clear.

"Oh, hell yeah, we're doing this at the station," she said, holding up a finger and wagging it at them. "You want to be on the books, fine. This will be written large all over your official record."

She raised her phone, but Dawson snatched it way. "What the *ever-loving fuck?*"

Dawson looked at her as if she was stupid. "Can't have you texting your boss or McLachlan about this. Trust me, sweetheart, you're going to want to talk to me first."

Maggie made a fist, making a concerted effort not to kick the potbellied detective in the nuts. "I'm texting my friend Peyton to cancel lunch."

"Here, give it to me." Jason took the phone and nodded. "It is to her friend."

Jason turned to her. "I can make you pancakes now, upstairs. We don't need to go to the C-6. Please, let's just do this here."

Maggie flushed, her jaw tight. "Get out your damn car and drive me to the police station. And give me my fucking phone back so I can text Peyton. She worries."

"Is Peyton the other one in the pictures?" Dawson whispered in an aside to Ethan as she and Jason stared at each other.

Ethan muttered something that sounded like yes. Jason handed her phone back. Turning her back on him, she wiped out the pancake message.

Peyton, don't tell my brothers, but I need you to find our family lawyer and have her meet me at precinct C-6. I'm being dragged in for questioning. It's about Calen.

The text reply came back immediately.

OMFG! Is Jason there? Can't he help?

Disgusted, she shook her head and typed. *He's part of it.*

Blinking back tears, she dropped the phone in her purse.

"I'm ready."

CHAPTER 8

Maggie stared down at the pictures Dawson had laid in front of her, undecided on whether to laugh or cry.

Despite her difficulty accepting that it was actually happening, she was sitting in an interrogation room at precinct C-6. She had been led by the arm—no cuffs—by Dawson through an entire room of police officers at their desks. Jason and Ethan trailed behind them. Looking wasted, Jason sat across from her. Dawson was beside her while Ethan held up the wall next to the door.

Dawson, the overbred turd of a man, had been following Calen and his associates for months now. There were snaps of her and Calen at various nightspots and some of the public spaces of the Caislean—sometimes with her brothers and sometimes without. Peyton was also in the pictures, as well as some of Siren's regulars and certain repeat guests at the hotel. Dawson even knew who her brothers were, but, somehow, he had never bothered to put a name to her face or any of the other women—with a few notable exceptions.

"Lisa is a prostitute?" she asked when Dawson pointed the woman out with a smug flourish.

She didn't know Lisa well, but Maggie wasn't all that surprised. The woman was what Peyton referred to as a professional girlfriend. A beautiful blonde, Lisa was frequently on the arm of a rich man. She liked to stay at the Caislean, although the registration was never in her name.

While the fact that the woman had a record was news, Maggie didn't care. Lisa was presentable and polite, and she had never been disruptive.

Discretion was a byword when one ran a hotel. By and large, she and her brothers let the guests live their own lives. The staff only got involved in clear-cut cases, when they knew someone was being harmed or exploited in some way. Such instances were rare. As for Lisa and the few others like her, Maggie thought they were strong enough to make their own decisions. She was a firm believer in the rights of sex workers. In her opinion, it was the Johns who needed to be punished.

When she looked back at Dawson, he was giving her one of those infuriatingly condescending looks again. "As if you didn't know—as if you aren't one, too."

Maggie stared in disbelief. "You...you think *I'm* a prostitute?" She lifted her stunned gaze to Jason.

"We know you work for these men," Dawson said, waving a picture of Liam with Calen in her face. "We have strong evidence that Calen McLachlan is running a prostitution ring out of the Caislean hotel with the owner's blessing—most likely because he's taking a cut. And you, my dear, are their go-between."

She was stunned, not just by the stupidity of the claim, but also by the lack of research this supposed professional hadn't done. *He doesn't even know Liam is my brother.*

"What kind of fucked-up sexist bullshit is this? You go to the trouble to find out who the men are in your pictures, but not the women? Did Jason not tell you my last name?"

Dawson leaned forward, his nose wrinkled. "I know everything I need to know. Right now, I have enough to charge you with solicitation. Is that what you want?"

"The *hell* you do." This time she did laugh, but she couldn't look at Jason. If she did, she would start to cry and she wasn't about to give him the satisfaction.

Dawson was starting to lose his temper. "Hey, you trumped-up—"

"All right, enough," Jason snapped at Dawson. "I'm getting her out of here."

"You agreed to let him make his offer," Ethan hissed at him.

"His offer is bullshit," Maggie interrupted. "Because the whole thing is bullshit! It's a fantasy dreamed up by a narrow-minded sexist jackass who doesn't do his fucking research."

Jason held up a hand. "I tried to tell you that I don't care if you were involved with McLachlan in the past, but...but if he's holding something over you, I want to get you out from under it. First, can you explain what is it that you think Dawson missed, because I'm not sure I understand," he said, his forehead creased.

"Neither do I. I don't understand how you could even think any of this is true. And seriously, how could you not tell him my fucking name?"

"What the hell does your name matter?" Dawson shouted.

"Because it's Tyler, you idiot," she yelled back. Maggie snatched the picture of Liam and Calen up and held it for them to see. "As in Liam Tyler, Patrick Tyler, and *Mary Margaret Tyler*—the co-owners of the Caislean hotel."

Silence.

She glared at Jason. "And yes, I know Calen. I've known him my entire life. He's been Liam's best friend since age five. When Calen's mother died, he practically moved in with us, up until my own parents passed away. He is like a brother to me. I consider him family. The fact that you think he and I were—blech. It's disgusting. You're disgusting. It would be like incest."

Someone swore under their breath. She thought it was Ethan, because Jason wasn't moving. He looked shocked and very pale. *Good. Serves him right.*

Maggie turned back to Dawson. "Now if I've cleared that up and you're done trotting out your baseless lies about my family, I'm going to leave—as much as I would like to stay and watch you further damage your career. Believe me, it would be more fun to wait for my lawyer and watch her tear you apart. And she would really enjoy it. The hotel's legal matters are usually fairly dull compared to this farce."

There was a knock at the door. "Speak of the devil," Maggie said, looking at her watch.

The timing was right. Thirty minutes had elapsed since she'd texted Peyton to call in the cavalry. Noreen Campos, her family's lawyer, was a local. She would have rushed over here as soon as she got word.

Ethan opened the door, and a uniformed police officer rushed in. She whispered frantically in Dawson's ear. Though the young officer tried to pitch her tone so she wouldn't overhear, Maggie heard '*pissed off*' and '*huge man in a suit*'.

Oh, shit. Liam was here. She flicked her gaze to Jason, almost feeling sorry for him. She had to leave before her brother got ahold of him.

"I'm done here."

No one stopped her as she got up and exited the room. She had reached the bullpen when she heard Jason call after her.

"Maggie, wait—"

Jason didn't catch up to her. He got one step outside the door before being hauled off his feet and pinned to the wall.

She hadn't seen Liam waiting off to the side—a testament to the turmoil of her thoughts. Her brother was massive and hard to miss. And despite how well Jason would have done against Mikael, she didn't think he could take her brother.

Pivoting on her heel, she rushed to Liam and tugged on his arm—the one holding Jason by the neck. "Liam, put him down."

Liam was ferocious. He was the type of man who seemed to grow bigger when he was angry. At this moment, he towered over everyone else in the room. The fact that he could deal with her now ex-boyfriend one-handed while wearing a fine wool suit made it even more intimidating.

Maggie quickly checked that none of the officers had drawn their guns on her brother, but they hadn't moved. Apparently, the presence of not one, but two, of their lawyers was enough of a deterrent. Noreen had been joined by another one of their attorneys, a young man whose name escaped her. Also, the local cops probably didn't recognize Jason or Ethan...not enough to stick up for them in front of an oversized, pissed-off billionaire.

Liam dragged Jason's head toward him until his face was inches away. "If you ever come near my sister again, I will bury you so deep you'll never see daylight."

"I was wrong. I thought she needed help." Jason's voice sounded steady, but his show of bravado rang a little false considering he was unsuccessfully trying to pull away from Liam's grasp.

Ethan was smart enough to stay out of it.

"I know exactly what you thought," Liam hissed. "I repeat—stay the fuck away from my sister. And don't even think about coming to find her at the hotel. Security will throw you out on your ass."

With that, he released Jason with a little shove in Ethan's direction.

At least he hadn't thrown a punch. Maggie put a hand on her forehead. She was getting a stress headache. Drained and dejected, she let Liam usher her to the door where Peyton was waiting.

Maggie widened her eyes as her friend ushered her to Liam's town car. "I told you not to tell him," she said from behind gritted teeth with a significant nod at Liam, who had stepped aside to say goodbye to Noreen.

Peyton hugged her before pulling back and shaking her head. "I didn't. But you didn't just text me. You added to the group text about brunch. That's how Liam knew what was happening," she explained as they climbed into the backseat.

Well, that was just perfect. "Oh, God, does he know Dawson was threatening to arrest me for solicitation? Tell me quick!"

Peyton's grimace was answer enough. "The female officer told Liam and Noreen that Dawson was shaking down a prostitute for information. They made it seem like no big deal until Liam laid into her and the rest of the department. Noreen got in a few licks, too. Then the chief came running out, and Liam started in on him as well. I've never heard so many swear words all at once—and some of them were from Noreen."

Maggie's groan was cut short when Liam climbed into the driver's seat. The tears were already slipping past the corner of her eyes, but when he turned to give her his I-will-fix-everything-because-I-am-your-big-brother look, it grew ten times worse.

She blinked back more tears.

Liam's expression darkened. "Do you want me to go back in there and kick his ass? Cause I'll do it. I don't care if there's a roomful of armed cops in there. I will take that fucking asshole down. I almost called Calen to come with me when I got your text. He'll kick Jason's ass, too. And so will Trick when he gets back from Thailand. He's due back this afternoon."

Maggie rested her head on Peyton's shoulders and closed her eyes. "Just take me home."

CHAPTER 9

It had been six hours. Trick appeared to think that was enough time lying prostrate in bed, but he was dead wrong. It was entirely too soon for her to contemplate getting up. Like the true friend she was, Peyton understood that even if Trick didn't. Both were camped out in her room with buckets of ice cream courtesy of the hotel's room service, but Maggie wasn't hungry.

"So, I was a prostitute too?" Peyton asked.

Maggie could hear what sounded like Trick laughing in the background. It was hard to tell with the pillow over her head.

Trick had been genuinely outraged when Liam had explained what had happened. Although "explain" was a euphemism for the epic rant Liam had treated him to moment he had walked through the door. But once Liam had retreated to his office, Trick's natural good humor had returned.

"Yes," she replied. "We were high-class hookers, and Liam was running us from the hotel for Calen. The damning evidence was all those notes and flash drives I passed between the two for our joint events. Maybe that meant I was the madam, too. I don't know."

The bed shook a little with Peyton's involuntary laughter. Maggie poked her head out from under the pillow.

"I'm not laughing," Peyton denied, her mouth contorting to keep from smiling. "I'm not. Jason is evil, and he will be destroyed. Our revenge will be painful and bloody. Let's start planning."

Maggie put the pillow back on her head. "Later."

All she wanted to do was lie here and not think.

Trick cleared his throat. "We've received a formal apology from BDP. I even got a personal call from the chief of detectives, which is something considering it's Sunday. They admit Dawson was sloppy, and that he took a shot he shouldn't have taken. Copious amounts of groveling ensued."

She shrugged. "Men are idiots."

Her brother removed the pillow "I'm going to give you that one. Today, all men are idiots."

"You're a good brother."

Always modest, Trick grinned. "I'm the best brother...so how long are you going to do this whole staying-in-bed thing?"

He was still smiling when he asked, but she could tell he was nervous.

When their parents had died, Maggie had spent the better part of a week in bed. Nothing Trick had done convinced her to get out of it. That had been the first time in their relationship she hadn't followed where he led, like the pied piper. It had freaked him out. Now every time she had a cold or the flu, he pushed her to get up immediately. Sweet and simultaneously annoying, that was Trick.

She thought about it. "I need twenty-four hours."

His shoulders relaxed. "That's it? Excellent, excellent." He started for the door, but then hesitated and turned back. "To be clear, you'll be out of bed tomorrow, as in Monday the sixteenth?"

"Yes, Trick. Twenty-four hours. I promise."

Peyton waited until he was gone. "You're a good sister."

"Thanks...but you're going to do it, right?"

"Yes. I will have Sam or Jose put the cot in your office tonight. It'll be waiting for you tomorrow morning."

She put the pillow back over her head and held out her hand. "Best-friend pinky swear?"

Peyton curled her pinky around hers. "Best-friend pinky swear."

CHAPTER 10

It had been almost a week now, and Jason was starting to feel desperate. Maggie wasn't returning his phone calls, texts, or emails...and he didn't blame her. Given what he'd gone along with, what it had implied about her, he knew was going to have to grovel for forgiveness. Some women were worth that. Maggie was one of them.

But first, he had to get to her.

He'd been camped out in the coffee shop for days now, but she hadn't appeared. Jason paced inside, assessing the entrance of the Caislean across the street with an investigator's eye. While it had multiple entrances and exits, the exclusive nature of the hotel meant it had an extremely well-trained security staff.

Jason had already been turned away at the lobby four times. Flashing his badge hadn't helped. The men told him it was Liam Tyler's orders, and if he wanted to, he could take it up with their lawyer. One time, the lawyer had been waiting for him. Noreen Campos had delighted in telling him that if he trespassed one more time, they would contact his superiors at the agency.

He didn't care. Threats weren't about to stop him. He and Maggie belonged together. She was justifiably angry, but he would make it up to her. All he needed was a way to make her listen.

Now that he knew who he was dealing with, Jason had finally done his homework on Mary Margaret Tyler and her brothers.

Their wealth was staggering. Never in his wildest dreams had he imagined that Maggie could be so rich. It didn't mesh with his preconceived ideas about the uber-wealthy. His Maggie was kind, down to earth, and practical. She worked hard at her job, too. He was still a little fuzzy on the details of what she did, but he understood that it involved organizing conferences and conventions at the hotel chain. And that was likely just the start of her responsibilities since she was part owner.

After the revelation, he had considered walking away. Someone like Maggie would have rich and successful tycoons at her beck and call. She could do a lot better than him. Except—except they couldn't love her more than Jason did. When she forgave him, he was going to do anything and everything to make her happy.

Plus, he had something going for him that was bigger than this mess. Maggie loved him. He knew that—was certain. She wasn't the type to engage in casual sex. If she didn't love him, she would have never given herself to him. Intimacy meant something to a girl like her.

According to his sources, each of the Tylers had their own set of apartments on the top floor of the hotel, where they lived full time. That floor was divided between their rooms, offices, and a handful of penthouse suites reserved for the ultra-rich.

Getting into the hotel as a *persona non-grata* was a challenge in and of itself. Getting onto that top-floor family area was proving to be nearly impossible.

His first idea had been to max out his credit card and reserve one of those suites using some sort of disguise, but further research revealed that the two spaces were not connected. The only way to the family's personal suites and offices was through a single private elevator located behind the manager's office on the ground floor.

Maggie is literally my princess in a tower.

Ethan came back in from his reconnaissance walk around the block. "This is going to take some work, but it's not impossible. Aside from the lobby and back entrance, there's a VIP entrance. All of those have at least two guards. The fire exits are wired and the staff entrances are keycard entry. I think those are our best bet. If we can lift a card from one of the maids—"

Someone behind them laughed—a feminine giggle. Jason swung around, his heart in his throat. But it wasn't Maggie.

"*Peyton.*"

Maggie's best friend was wearing oversized sunglasses and a sweatshirt with the hood pulled over her dark hair. She tugged it down and lowered the shades to study him.

"And then what?" she asked.

He and Ethan stared at her.

She propped her head on her hands. "Only certain maids are authorized to work on the top floor, and their keycards only work in the hotel proper," Peyton informed them. "The elevator to the family offices has a thumbprint lock. Only the print from authorized personnel grants access to the inner sanctum."

"But you have access, don't you?" Ethan asked, turning on his megawatt smile for her.

"As a matter of fact, I do." Peyton grinned. "But that does you no good. The word came from on high. You aren't to get anywhere near Maggie. Liam's men would treat it like a hostage situation, and you'd end up in jail—he's a very protective older brother. Besides, you're assuming I want to help you. And after what you did, that's kind of a big if..."

"If you don't want to help, why are you here?" Ethan's smile had dimmed.

She gestured to Jason. "To see if he deserves an opportunity."

"What kind of opportunity?" Ethan asked, a corner of his mouth turning down.

"I don't care," Jason said eagerly, waving at him to shut up. He couldn't let his partner's naturally suspicious nature ruin this for him. That was how he'd landed in this mess in the first place.

"I know I'm an idiot," he told Peyton. "The biggest asshole in the world. Everything you've thought, I have already said to myself ten times over. I'm prepared to beg on hands and knees for another chance. In fact—I'll start now."

Jason knelt in front of her and put his hands together in prayer.

Peyton leaned back with a satisfied expression. "That's what I was waiting for."

She put a hand in her pocket and handed him a key card. "I sometimes freelance in the security department, so I can program these."

"I thought you said there was no key card access to her room," Jason said, taking it from her.

"There isn't. And I can't put you on the thumbprint lock without one of the Tylers signing off on it—and let me tell you now that is *not* going to happen. If this were the days of feudal lords, Liam would have you drawn and quartered. Even Trick is itching to kick your ass into next week."

Jason's lips compressed. "I'm aware. He told me so himself the second time security showed me to the door. So, what exactly does this open?" he asked, holding up the card.

A suspicious-looking grin played at the corner of Peyton's lips. Whatever was coming was trouble.

"Let me ask you something first. Maggie said you always vetoed going to the rooftop bars she suggested. And there was that incident with the glass elevator—you climbed six or seven flights to avoid riding in one. Was there a reason for that?"

Jason narrowed his eyes at her. "Yeah...*why?*"

The glint in Peyton's eye was downright devilish now. "Let's just say you're definitely going to earn this second chance."

CHAPTER 11

Maggie tried to study the contracts for the next series of conventions that would be held at the hotel, but it was hopeless. She rubbed her temples. The tension there was coalescing into a full-blown headache.

Her head was a maelstrom of emotion. Even though more than a week had passed and she had gotten out of bed the following day—as promised—she still felt unbalanced. Shock, surprise, anger, and indignation were all in competition to drive her crazy.

How the hell could Jason have believed she was a prostitute? *I guess it's true—some guys can't tell when a girl is a virgin.*

And that slimy detective. *Ugh*. Just remembering the way Dawson had threatened her, trying to compel her into giving up evidence on Calen. It made her furious all over again just thinking about it—as if she would ever do that. And even if she *had* agreed—had worn a wire every time she saw Calen for the next year—they would still have nothing because he wasn't a criminal. That was his father, a man Calen rarely saw and hardly ever spoke to. She certainly hadn't met him. Liam had made sure of that.

Anger soon turned to hurt. *Crap, shit, crap.*

Tears stung at her eyes. Maggie felt humiliated. She'd been so fixated and hopeful about Jason that she'd ascribed things to their relationship that didn't exist. Her fantasy man. God, she was such an idiot.

Except he wanted to save you. Or so he had said. He'd offered to run away with her. But how much had that been part of the effort to coerce her into turning informant? Had it been some twisted good-cop-bad-cop scenario?

And what if she *had* been a prostitute? Maggie was almost sure that offer would have been dust once she'd agreed to help Dawson.

Don't think about it anymore.

Forcing her attention back to her work, she signed a few memos, writing her signature with enough violence to rip the paper.

"Shit!" She was turning to her computer to print the contract again when a large shadow fell over her desk. Outside the hermetically sealed windows, the window-washing rig was slowly lowering into view.

Maggie shot out of her seat. "What the hell is going on?" she asked aloud.

Today was Monday. The windows were always cleaned on Thursdays, so they'd be ready for Friday night check-ins and the hotel's busier weekend traffic.

Her question was answered when the platform came to a rest outside her window, revealing the occupants inside. Julio, the window foreman, was there. He held the controls with his habitual smile, but his grin was a little broader than usual. In fact, he appeared to be laughing at someone lying on the floor of the rig.

Maggie put her head on the window, trying to make out the identity of the prone figure. Julio tugged on the stranger's jacket, and the other man raised his head.

"Jason! What the hell do you think you're doing?"

Her jerk of lover didn't answer. It was doubtful he could hear her through the thick glass. The entire hotel had the same noise-reducing panels. Maggie banged on the glass until he finally saw her.

Despite his unnatural shade of green, Jason pulled himself up until he was on his feet, facing her across the glass. Maggie bit her lip to keep from smiling as he held up a single bedraggled rose.

Snatching up a blank piece of paper from her printer, she scrawled a message on it.

SERIOUSLY! it read. She held it up to the glass.

Jason said something that looked like, "I'm sorry".

She picked up another piece of paper.

The windows are sealed AND soundproof.

Clutching the side of the rig like he thought it would fall out from under him, Jason pressed his head against the glass, fishing something out of his pocket and displaying it to her.

It was his phone. He typed something on it.

I'm afraid of heights.

Oh, good grief. *Then get back to the roof and go home,* she scrawled on the backside of the paper.

Not yet. I need to tell you how sorry I am.

Maggie glowered at him and grabbed more paper. *Did you really believe I was a prostitute?*

Jason winced. *Very briefly.*

She made a fist and banged the glass just over his face.

I'm sorry!

He pulled the phone back and started typing furiously again. *I was stupid to believe Dawson, but everything I said to you just before was true. I thought I was helping you. The idea of you under the thumb of someone like Dawson described scared the shit out of me. Please meet me on the roof. I have more to say, but I can't stay out here.*

Jason was staring at her face, into her eyes. Though he was no longer a sickly green shade, his free hand—the one not holding the phone—was clutching the railing with a white-knuckled grip. His expression pleaded with her.

"Fine!" she shouted and pointed at the ceiling. Jason motioned behind him, and Julio turned the controls to lift the platform up to the roof.

She took the elevator and found Trick waiting at the roof's access door. He was almost jumping up and down, a gleeful expression on his face.

"What are you doing here?"

"Julio has been live-tweeting this spectacle. I imagine half the staff is on their way to the roof."

Maggie swore and hurried outside. Her breath caught as she saw there were already at least two dozen people on the roof with more coming up the stairs behind them.

Why the hell is Julio's Twitter account so damn popular?

"You are going to forgive him, aren't you?" her brother asked from behind her.

She swung around to face him. "I thought you were in the let's-have-Jason's-guts-for-garters camp."

"That's Liam. After I saw this, I felt for the guy." Trick handed over his phone. There was a picture of Jason. His eyes were squeezed tightly shut and he was sitting on the floor of the rig, holding on to his single rose with one hand and the railing with the other. His face was white, his lips pinched at the corners.

"Any guy who gets on a window-washing rig on a forty-story building when he's afraid of heights deserves another shot."

Maggie swore a blue streak and kicked the outside of the access door. "Damn it! He does, doesn't he?"

Trick laughed. "I think so, but Liam doesn't agree. He keeps texting me to have security throw him out again. Jason is lucky he's in Lisbon this week." His phone went off again, but he put it in his pocket.

"Does he follow Julio too?" she asked.

"Everybody does. Julio takes the best selfies from the rig and does a weekly caption contest."

Trick nudged her. "There are more roses," he stage-whispered, pointing to the side of the building. A few members of the hotel staff were holding bouquets, a least six or seven of them.

"He probably spent half his paycheck on those," her brother mused. "I just looked up average salaries for FBI agents last week. It's not a lot."

"Can you not ruin this romantic moment for me?" she asked in exasperation, swinging back around when people started shouting.

The slow-moving platform had made it back up to the roof. Julio waved to the crowd like an English royal in a parade while a few men went to open the door. Jason stumbled out like he'd come from inside of one their industrial-sized washing machines, set on high.

He landed on his knees and quickly sat down on the roof, his back to the railing. He wasn't looking at her or the crowd. Both his hands were covering his face as he tried to get his bearings.

Maggie flushed, aware that everyone was looking at her. For a split second, she wanted to ask everyone to leave, but she couldn't do that. Most of these people had been with them for years—ever since her brothers had opened their first hotel. They had watched her grow up. Antonio, their concierge, had taught her how to drive. Maria Elena, one of the housekeepers, had been the one to explain what tampons were for. Maria Elena's sister Constanza had taken her shopping for her first bra. They had been there for all her big moments. It seemed right that they should be here for this one, as embarrassing as it was.

Taking a deep breath, she looked neither right nor left until she was in front of Jason. She crouched down in front of him, and then tugged his hands off his eyes.

"You, sir, are a prize idiot."

Jason's tight expression eased. He looked so happy to see her that her heart soared.

"I know. I'm sorry." His voice was like sandpaper.

"I can't believe you did that if you're afraid of heights," she said, gesturing behind him to the rig.

"I needed to let you know how much I love you, and there wasn't another way...so do you think you can give me another chance?"

Maggie pursed her lips, very aware of their audience...and that he had just told her he loved her. "Don't get me wrong—I appreciate the big gesture, but you monumentally screwed up."

"Does that mean you don't want this?" he asked, holding out the sadly mangled red rose.

"Oh, I want it, *and* you. However, I think you need to look around." She gestured to the crowd of hotel staff. "It's not just my brothers who will unleash a can of whoop-ass on you if you screw up again. It's all these people too—they are my family. So you better watch your step."

Jason didn't seem to care about the implied threat. His grin was irrepressible. "I can handle that. I can handle anything as long as you love me back."

She leaned in closer. "Good. And in case it wasn't clear—I do love you too."

"Maggie?"

"Yes?"

"That is the best Christmas present anyone has ever gotten me."

Maggie's mouth dropped open. He was right. It was Christmas Eve. In her distraction, she'd forgotten.

Jason laughed and put his hands on either side of her face to pull her in for a kiss. The moment their lips touched, she forgot all about their audience and the fact they were on a very windy rooftop. Her entire world was that simple, sweet touch of his lips on hers.

Jason broke off first. He was laughing, and it took her a moment to realize why. The sound she had thought was the wind picking up was their audience. They were cheering and clapping in approval.

"I guess it's going to be a big wedding," he said.

Maggie put her hand over her mouth and laughed, tears stinging at her eyes before she wiped the smile from her face. "Who said I was going to marry you?"

Jason stopped smiling. "*Me*. I did. You *are* going to marry me."

He was right.

CHAPTER 12

ONE YEAR LATER

"It goes without saying that if you hurt my baby sister, I will kill you."

Jason rolled his eyes. "Hell, Liam. You have to do this right now?" He nodded at the gathering crowd.

Liam didn't even blink. "I think now is the perfect time."

Jason had to give it to the guy. Maggie's oldest brother had a single-track mind and the kind of persistence empires were founded on.

"Well, I guess I get the symbolism of the timing and everything, but it's not like this isn't well-covered territory," he said, giving his best man, Ethan, the side-eye.

Ethan shrugged. He probably considered threatening to kill the groom a rite of passage. His partner was traditional that way.

"Did I or did I not sign the damn prenup you shoved at me?" Jason asked, keeping his eyes peeled on the doorway.

Technically, Maggie wasn't late yet...but she wasn't early either.

Liam conceded that with a nod. "You did. But that's not the same thing as not arguing with Maggie."

Jason smirked at the way he was losing ground. "So now we can't even fight?"

"You can fight; you just have to let her win."

"Maggie would lose all respect for me if I let her win all the time." She usually destroyed him in arguments anyway. It was all those years of quarreling with her brothers. She was well-trained. The girl was devious and too smart for her own good.

God, he loved her.

"Don't forget our deal. I signed the damn prenup on the condition that you don't tell Maggie about it. She'll be mad at me for signing it... and even madder at you for having it made up in the first place."

Jason honestly didn't care. He had no intention of ever getting divorced, so whatever Liam wanted him to sign was fine with him. If it made Maggie's brother get off his case, it was worth it. Of course, it hadn't worked completely. Case in point—this pre-wedding pep talk.

"When is Maggie getting here?" he asked, looking at his watch.

It wasn't like she had far to go. The wedding ceremony was on the Caislean's roof.

Maggie had wanted the hotel's employees to help decide the theme of their ceremony. True to form, Julio, window-washing supervisor and social-media genius, had set up an online poll. "The Hanging Gardens of Babylon" had been the clear winner, mainly because everyone had gotten caught up in the idea of having the ceremony on the roof where he had professed his love.

The staff had gone nuts transforming the previously barren space into a gorgeous rooftop garden. The Christmas accents added another dimension to the magical scene. Maggie had taken one look and insisted they keep it that way all year round. The only space that competed with it was the grand ballroom on the ground floor, where their reception would take place later.

Of course, if Maggie didn't show up, he might throw himself off this beautiful roof. "How late is she now?'

Ethan laughed. "She's not late yet."

Liam sighed. "She'll show. Maggie's not a welcher."

With that, Liam turned to look at him again. "You'll be a good husband. Give it a few decades and I'll tear up the prenup."

"Aww," Jason said as he punched Liam in the shoulder. "Hey, man, I'm touched." That was about as warm as his soon-to-be brother-in-law was ever liable to get.

"Yeah, yeah," Liam growled. "It's not like our lawyers couldn't tear you apart without one."

Jason laughed. Liam was really starting to warm up to him.

Further conversation was suspended when Trick ran upstairs. He signaled the string quartet.

Seconds later, Jason saw her. Mary Margaret Tyler, the love of his life, was walking toward him. Everything in him relaxed, and he breathed a sigh of relief.

Next to him, Liam sighed too. "Have lots of babies...but, you know, not soon."

This time, Ethan laughed.

Jason smacked Liam in the back. "Shut up already and go get your sister. Walk her down the aisle fast. I can't wait to be married to her."

For once, Liam didn't argue.

CHAPTER 13

Maggie threw her coat on the chair and rushed into the bedroom to take off her clothes. While she was excited to go to Calen's for dinner, she was even more excited to see Jason, her husband, during the one-hour break he had tonight.

Jason was deep in an investigation, his first major case since returning from their honeymoon a month ago. Maggie worried about him, but she knew Jason was more than capable of looking out for himself.

It helped that his transfer to the white-collar division was now permanent. He and Ethan had managed to make their mark there and both were on track for promotions, despite the snafu with Dawson. They enjoyed the work, which was more challenging and mentally stimulating than dangerous—which suited her just fine. She didn't need to be married to an action junky, but she was proud that, through his efforts, Jason made a difference in the lives of people who'd lost everything to swindlers and scammers.

In the end, Dawson didn't suffer much from the attempt to coerce her into cooperating with his ill-conceived crusade. After getting reamed by his superiors for shoddy investigative techniques, he voluntarily resigned from the BPD. Last she heard, he'd landed a cushy job in the private sector.

After the mess with Dawson had been cleared up, Jason had set a few rules about their association with Calen McLachlan, scion of one of Boston's biggest criminal syndicates. Maggie was free to socialize with him as often as she pleased. Jason didn't want to dictate any of the parameters of her friendships. But he also didn't go out of his way to hang out with Calen himself. He and Ethan kept their distance. Jason had no desire to be dragged into any investigations against him, especially since he'd finally accepted that the man had zero criminal aspirations.

Of course, there was one less-than-noble thing Jason did every time she was scheduled to dine at Calen's place…something she couldn't bring herself to give him a hard time about. Not when it brought her so much pleasure.

"You better be naked!" Jason yelled from the doorway.

Maggie tossed away her shirt. "I'm more naked than you. I beat you here by two whole minutes."

"Except I started undressing in the hallway," Jason said, bursting into the bedroom in his boxer shorts and shirtsleeves.

"Jason!" She giggled. "There are cameras out there. Your pants better not be too."

He grinned unrepentantly. "We could always move to my old place. The security cameras there are just for show. Besides—Samuel and Ortiz in the security office always high-five me when they catch us doing something nasty on the hotel feed."

Oh no, she hoped those two didn't mention that little detail to her brothers. She shimmied out of her skirt. "Well, I hoped they enjoyed the show."

She was about to add more, but her mind went blank when her husband stripped out of his shirt and shorts.

"*Damn.*"

Maggie would never grow tired of Jason's gold-dusted beauty. Even when they were old and gray and he no longer had those defined biceps or that six-pack, she could spend the rest of her life staring into his eyes or listening to his stories.

Then again, as long as he did have those rock-hard abs—she would enjoy them as often as she could.

Maggie was about to demand that he get in bed when he rushed over. He took hold of her face, kissing her breathless before lifting her off her feet.

She landed on the bed with a bounce only to be immediately flipped on her stomach. Seconds later, her bra was unclasped and her panties stripped off. Jason's hand moved between her legs only to find she was more than ready.

"I love how wet you always are for me," he murmured, tracing patterns on her silky inner lips.

Maggie hummed happily and pushed back against his hand. "You're wasting time."

Never one to keep a lady waiting, Jason hauled on her hips, pulling her onto her knees so abruptly her backside met his thighs with a little slap.

His already-hard cock teased her folds, little sparks that fed her hunger.

Moaning, Maggie wiggled her backside in a silent plea to be taken. Jason tsked and spanked her. "What have I told you? Dirty things come to those who wait."

She wanted to argue about the amount of time they had left, but he chose the moment to run his hands up her rib cage, rubbing and palming her breasts before pinching her nipples.

Already on the brink, Maggie nearly sobbed in relief when Jason covered her, the skin of his chest against her back. One of his hands went in her hair, twisting it around his hand. He pulled it slightly and brought his lips to her ear.

"Is this what you want…or do you want more?"

"More," she gasped. "I want more."

"Good."

Keeping her pinned against him with his hold on her hair, Jason used his free hand to pull her hips, aligning the entrance of her channel with his cock. Throwing her head back, she opened her mouth in a silent scream as his thick shaft breached her body. Her aching flesh welcomed him home as he buried himself in her.

Desperate, she fisted her hands in the bed as he pistoned in and out, a cataclysmic force that swept her up, driving her higher and higher.

Too impatient to keep her on her hands and knees, Jason put an arm around her waist and flipped them around. He landed on his back with her draped over him like a silk sheet. Maggie tried to turn around to face him, but he kept her on her back, effortlessly pinning her against him with a forearm under her breasts. He tucked the other arm under her knees so she was helpless, unable to move, while he thrust again and again.

Maggie arched and writhed, moaning as her husband's thick member drove her out of her mind. Holding him tight, she threw one arm behind her, trying to wrap it around his head as his next thrust triggered a supernova. As she shuddered and shook, she felt Jason's arms come around her as he held her through the maelstrom. Moments later, his cock throbbed and jerked. He ground against her, extending her orgasm until all her muscles seized and then relaxed, She stretched over him, spent and sated.

Long minutes later, Jason hummed. "That should keep you."

Maggie laughed and smacked his shoulder. "For now," she conceded. "Mmm...I wish I could stay here all night."

"Why don't you? I have to go back and relieve Ethan, but you don't have to go to Calen's for dinner."

Maggie suppressed a smile at the hopeful note in his voice. "But I don't want to. I have to meet his houseguest."

Jason grunted, his hand stroking the skin of her midriff. "I forgot about the mystery houseguest."

"Liam says Calen is going to marry her."

Underneath her, Jason froze. "Really?"

"Uh-huh. Trick says she's very sweet. She's a grad student or something."

She couldn't see his face, but, somehow, she could feel Jason's glee.

"Is that so? Well, that's great news!"

As much as she hated to lose the feel of him inside her, Maggie shifted, letting his now-soft cock slip out of her body so she could roll to the side. "Does this mean you're going to stop sexing me up every time I go over to Calen's?"

The dumbfounded expression on his face was priceless. Jason's mouth closed. "I don't know what you're talking about."

Amused, she propped her head on her hand and widened her eyes at him. "You're going to deny the fact that every time I join my brothers for dinner at Calen's, you make sure to fuck my brains out first?"

"And why would I do that?" he asked cautiously.

"Oh, I don't know. Could it be that you want to make sure I'm so sexually satisfied I'll never give Calen a second look?"

He narrowed his eyes at her. "Okay. When did you realize what I was up to?"

"Hmm. Let's see. It was probably right after we got engaged and I had to go to Siren to talk to Calen about a party there. You made a lot of noise about enjoying a night in, watching boxing, but before I went out the door, you went down on me for like an hour."

Jason shook his head. "It was not an hour."

"Well, it *felt* like an hour. Thank you for that by the way," she added with a giggle before leaning over and resting her head on his chest. "I don't know why you would think my feelings for him would ever change. You know he's like blood to me. "

"Yeah, yeah. So you keep saying. But…"

"What?"

"Well, Liam is like a brother to Peyton, and she…"

She shrugged. "I'm not Peyton."

Jason groaned. "Why couldn't your dangerous and wealthy surrogate brother look like Steve Buscemi or Ron Perlman? You know, something reasonable?"

Her laughter shook the bed.

After a minute, Jason sighed and put a hand behind his head. "Why didn't you tell me you'd figured me out?"

Maggie gave him her most impish smile. "And why would I do that when the benefits of letting you go on were so damn good?"

Jason spanked her, hard. She could feel herself growing wet again.

"Your brothers are right; you *are* a brat."

"Too late. You already married me. Now you're stuck with me for life."

He turned and pinned her underneath him. "Good. I'm planning on making every day count."

She wrapped her arms around his neck. "Hmm. I think I'm going to be late for dinner."

The End

Need another obsession? Try Codename Romeo

Encountering a tiny toddler alone in the hall changes everything for FBI agent Ethan Thomas. Relief sets in when the child's mother appears. But when she collapses at his feet just before a blizzard hits Boston, Ethan's in over his head.

FIND this and the rest of Lucy's award-winning books using the QR codes above!

BONUS STORY

THE HEX, A SPELLBOUND REGENCY PREQUEL SHORT

CHAPTER 1

Moira ran headlong over the barren cliffs, the weight of her skirts slowing her down. The distant sound of dogs barking behind her sent a bolt of fear shooting up her spine. She could barely breathe, but she had to keep going or she was going to die.

You're already dead.

She had sealed her own fate through her rage. Her former fiancé, Duncan, might never walk again, and he had lost the use of his right eye forever.

It wasn't supposed to be this way. Right now she and Duncan were supposed to be on their honeymoon in the English countryside. Instead, he was maimed and she was being pursued by his father, Boyd Fraser, and his men.

Don't forget the dogs.

She lifted up her skirts, and then mentally tried to reach inside herself, tapping reserves she didn't know she had. Putting one foot in front of the other, she forced herself on, stumbling occasionally over a rock or hole.

She should have never agreed to marry Duncan. He'd come to her village with a group of men doing business with the village elders. She had been infatuated with him from the start and was flattered when he seemed equally taken with her. He had come back to see her several times over the course of the next few months. She'd been foolish enough to believe he loved her when really all he'd wanted was her small dowry.

Her mother, Helen, had never approved of Duncan. Moira should have listened to her, but she'd been blind to the warning signs, intent only on her romance. He proposed a few months after meeting, and she wouldn't hear a word against him. Despite her mother's protests, she had left Carrbridge to marry a near stranger. She had never spoken to her mother again.

Moira had followed Duncan to this home village of Stonehaven, believing their marriage was only days away. Then in a blink of an eye it had all been over. Duncan had come to her and broken their engagement, explaining that he'd found another girl with a bigger dowry and that he never wanted to see her again.

She had been devastated by Duncan's defection, but might have been able to forgive him for breaking the engagement if it hadn't been for what followed.

The day after Duncan had come to see her she was asked to leave the room she had let at the local boarding house. The landlord had told her that they didn't want her kind of woman there. When she asked what kind of woman she was supposed to be, they told her soiled goods had no right to mix with decent people.

Moira had died inside when she heard that. It wasn't enough that Duncan had forsaken her; he'd had to destroy her reputation too.

Her love had turned to hate and she'd struck out, determined to hurt him as much as he'd hurt her. Her magic had always been used to heal, to concoct salves and potions that helped the weak and the sick. But betrayal had made it a weapon.

The hex she'd mixed up was meant to inflict pain—the same pain Duncan had dealt her times three. She'd wanted him to suffer, to give him a memory of fear and anguish that he would carry for the rest of his life. But he wasn't supposed to be permanently harmed.

She had underestimated her own rage. The emotion she'd channeled into her spell had overwhelmed it. When Duncan was struck down, his body hadn't been able to contain the force of her anger. His

BONUS STORY

leg had broken in two places with the violent contortions, and he'd managed to claw at one eye—partially blinding himself—before members of his family had tied him down. They dosed him with enough laudanum to make him insensible, but not before he'd whispered in his father's ear, giving Boyd Fraser her name because she'd been fool enough to tell her fiancé what she was.

When everything had gone wrong, Moira had fled to a cheap inn. Boyd's men had come for her early that morning. If she had been asleep in her bed, it would already be too late. However, the unfamiliar noises of the coaching inn had woken her well before dawn. She'd heard them coming and had jumped out of the narrow ground floor window, hurtling past the morning bustle in the courtyard and toward the cliffs near Stonehaven.

The landscape was different from Carrbridge. Here on the coast the plants were sparse and scraggly from too much salt air. There were no trees to hide behind. Her only hope was to stay ahead of the dogs. If she could only stop, she might remember a spell to divert the animals and help her hide. But there was no time.

Even if she had a chance to escape, she didn't deserve it. Moira had broken the most important rule her mother had taught her about her gift—to do no harm. Their magic was meant to heal, to help the sick and ease the torment of those poor unfortunates beyond their skill. Moira had forgotten that in her pain. Maybe she did deserve to die because of it.

Nevertheless, she couldn't stop and surrender herself to Boyd. It had only taken one meeting to know that he was a man without a mercy. She shuddered to think what he would do to her if he caught her.

Her only option was to escape in a manner of her own choosing. The rocky cliffs were high above the shore. With luck, she would die instantly. Especially if her head struck one of the many rocks littering the water's edge. It would be a kinder death than letting Boyd get his hands on her.

Don't think about it. Whatever you do, don't think. Keep moving.

Tears ran down her face when she thought of never seeing her family again. Not her mother or sister. And she wouldn't be there to watch her niece, a brilliant little girl with hair the same color as her own, grow into womanhood. Her life was over, all her dreams shattered by her own hand.

Ahead of her, the uneven ground ended abruptly. Beyond it there was nothing but sky. *The cliffs.* Slowing down, she leaned on a tall boulder a few feet from the edge. Her limbs were shaking, the muscles in her legs twitching and leaping independently as she struggled to stay on her feet.

She was bent nearly double when she rounded the tall rock—which was why she didn't see the man waiting on the other side.

When his arms came up around her, trapping her against his chest, she couldn't scream. That required air in her lungs. Instead, her legs gave way and she slumped over in defeat.

I've failed.

How was she going to die? Would they hang her? Burn her at the stake?

"Moira, look at me."

The voice was familiar, although the accent was jarring. She cracked open an eyelid and met the pale blue eyes of Nigel Smythe, Duncan's English cousin. He was a poor relation of the Fraser family, up for a visit before he moved away from his home in the north of England, although she couldn't remember the reason for the move. Moira had only met him once, shortly after arriving in Stonehaven with Duncan.

Nigel was a minister in his country. He was supposed to officiate their wedding. No doubt he would be asked to preside over the new one if Duncan's new fiancée was still willing to have him.

"Let me go," she pleaded, deciding to throw herself on his mercy. "I'm going over the cliffs. I will never hurt anyone again, I promise. Just let me go."

Nigel's pale handsome face contorted in a sympathetic wince. "I can't do that. You see, I'm here to save you."

CHAPTER 2

The inside of the hired carriage was very dark. She sat in the corner of the bench, trying to ignore the jostling movement while she studied Nigel sitting across from her.

"I did it."

Perhaps she shouldn't have admitted that, but he didn't look surprised.

"I know," he said quietly.

"Then why are you helping me?" she asked, despite being afraid to hear the answer.

Nigel looked away, his attention fixed on the small sliver of rolling green that was visible between the gap in the curtains. He had a handsome face now that she was looking at him. But there hadn't been much of a reason to before. Not when Duncan had been in the room.

Nigel was slighter than his cousin, his features just as defined and attractive, but in a setting so pale as to look ghostly. His ice blue eyes were nearly colorless in the weak light, and his pale blond hair did little to call attention to the fineness of his visage. His coloring combined with his quiet manner ensured he would blend in at gatherings.

When he didn't answer, she repeated her question.

"I'm not sure," he said finally.

"For what it's worth, it wasn't supposed to be that severe. I just wanted to hurt him as badly as he hurt me." She paused. "Don't you want to punish me? Burn me alive? You're a man of the cloth. It's what you're supposed to do."

"I...I believe that God put people like you on this earth for a reason. And it's not to be an evil we must fight."

That sounded like he'd had experiences with others of her kind. "Have you met anyone with magic before?"

He nodded. "There was an old man who lived outside my village. We...used to throw stones at his house. When I grew into manhood that troubled me. It still does. He was harmless."

"I'm not," she whispered.

His eyes narrowed. "No, you're not. But you won't hurt anyone again, will you?"

"No," she admitted.

Her guilt was flaying her alive, and he could probably see it. She couldn't live with herself if she harmed someone again.

"They won't stop looking for me," she warned him.

"Uncle thinks you're dead."

Her eyes widened.

"When you changed into the clothing I brought you, I tore your old dress and took pieces of it down to the bottom of the cliff. Part of it will be caught in the rocks along with some blood. A larger part will be found in the water, if at all."

Her mouth fell open. "Whose blood is it?"

"A pigeon."

"Oh."

"I didn't kill it," he said with an ironic twist to his lips. "I bought it from the butcher, fresh this morning. He thought I was making a pie."

He had spent a considerable amount of time on the details.

"You thought of everything."

He frowned and shrugged. "I had all night to plan after Uncle Boyd gathered his friends. He expected me to come with him this morning, but I told him my patron had recalled me."

"Your patron?"

"The Viscount Anders. He has given me a living in my hometown, near the border, but I am going to ask him for on farther away, on his southernmost property."

"Why?"

He stared at her for a long moment. "Because, although my Scottish relations would have little reason to visit me in Northumberland, they will definitely not be visiting as far south as Eastbourne...so they would have little reason to meet my wife."

"Your *wife*?"

Color crept up into his pale cheeks. "It's one idea. If you would prefer to strike out on your own, I can help you disappear. You can travel with me as far as London, and I can give you a little money to help you on your way."

"I thought you didn't have any," she said quietly, staring at him in wonderment.

Why would he offer marriage after what she had done?

His fingers drummed on the seat next to him. "I'm not wealthy. Not compared to my cousin," he admitted. "My father was a fourth son, but I have a little saved. I realize that your prospects were considerably higher before Duncan came into your life. I couldn't offer you riches, but you would have a home and eventually a family."

Feeling slightly dizzy, she sat up straighter. "Don't you believe I'm going to burn in the fires of Hell for witchcraft?"

"Duncan will live," he said, in a tone that suggested he wasn't sure if he was happy about it. "His leg was set yesterday. He may be lame and will most likely require the use of a cane, but he will live. You didn't kill anyone. Even his eye may recover. Only time will tell."

More relieved than she could say, she nodded and then slumped slightly in her seat. Her throat was thick, and her eyes stung. "That still doesn't explain why you would sacrifice yourself to marry me. You're a man of the cloth, and I'm a witch. Don't you believe I'm damned?"

He coughed slightly and turned very red. "I don't believe God would create something so beautiful and make it evil."

Her stomach gave a funny little flutter. "You think I'm beautiful?" she asked slowly.

His smile was a touch too wry for a minister. "My cousin would hardly propose to a homely woman. Although his new fiancée is only passable, in my opinion, but I suppose her considerable fortune enhances her charms."

Moira's brows drew down. "You're not like any priest I've ever met before."

"I'm a minister, not a priest. Although, if I'd had the funds, I would have been a gentleman farmer instead." He paused. "Also, I believe Duncan behaved very dishonorably. Even if he'd come to the realization that he no longer wished to continue the engagement, he never should have admitted that he had...that you...had..."

Shame flooded through her. *He knew.* Of course, everyone did. She was a fool to believe otherwise.

"And you still want to marry me?"

A would-be husband had the right to expect a virgin on his wedding night. That a man of the cloth would willingly marry a woman who had lost her honor—it was unthinkable.

"Yes," he said simply, his pale eyes gleaming with a silver edge.

Something about that look made her very warm inside. Sure that her blushing face matched her hair, she looked away. Dropping her eyes down to her lap, she admitted something she hadn't wanted to acknowledge, even to herself.

"I didn't want to," she whispered so quietly her voice was barely audible over the sound of the horses' hoofbeats.

Duncan hadn't forced himself on her, but he also hadn't given her much of a choice. He'd said it didn't matter because they were going to be married soon anyway, and then wouldn't let her leave the room at the inn unless she submitted to him. Rationalizing that he was right, she would soon be his wife, she had allowed herself to be pressured into acting against her own judgment. It hadn't been a pleasant experience, and remembering it now made her angry all over again.

When she finally looked at Nigel, he was watching her sorrowfully. "I figured it was something like that. I am very sorry. But there are things that I know about my cousin that you do not. You see there was this other young lady, very poor and pretty. I...I think he got what he deserved."

So many things suddenly made sense. Had Nigel loved this girl? Why else had he been willing to save her, crossing his own family? Reading the stiffness in his expression, the firm set of his lips, she knew her guess was true. He had loved another girl. And he had lost her.

Was this poor and pretty girl dead? Moira guessed that she was, or Nigel would be married to her now. He was that kind of man. That was as clear to her as daylight. She could feel his goodness with every fiber of her being.

Why hadn't she had this kind of insight about Duncan? She could have spared herself so much heartache simply by staying away. Shutting her eyes, she pushed away the painful regret. It hurt too much to dwell upon what might have been. This was her new reality.

She was going to be Nigel's wife. Even if he was simply doing it to get back at his cousin, or if she was to be a replacement for the woman he had lost, this was her best option. Perhaps in time, she could repay him for his kindness.

"I don't want to disappear," she said. "I would prefer to marry you, if you're certain that's what you want."

He didn't look pleased exactly. It was more like satisfaction, but there was only a brief flash of emotion and then he sobered.

"I should warn you it will not be easy. We won't have many comforts. The living down south is rather small. And there is another thing to consider—you won't be able to contact your family. Not ever. My uncle Boyd is a vindictive man. If your family knew you were alive, he would hurt them to find you."

Oh Lord, he was right, she realized with a sickening pang. She could not endanger her loved ones in that way. Not on top of the shame her actions had already caused them. As it was, they might not want to speak to her again, anyway.

The carriage hit a bump, and she braced herself against the wall before answering. "I understand," she said hoarsely and then tried to decide what else to say. How did one thank a man for saving your life?

"I will try to be a good wife."

A corner of Nigel's mouth quirked before he stepped across the carriage to seat himself next to her. He held out his hand. Tentatively she reached out and touched his palm with her fingers. His hand closed around hers.

"I believe you," he said quietly.

CHAPTER 3

Moira hung the clean sheets on the line, savoring the sun on her face. Though she missed Scotland, this little hamlet near Eastbourne was like some sort of dream. The weather was so much warmer in southern England, and the sun shone so often they could hang the wet linens outside this late in the year.

Though it was out of necessity, Moira didn't mind doing the washing herself. They only had a cook and a part time maidservant, but she enjoyed contributing to the housework. Working hard kept her mind occupied. It helped alleviate some of the guilt she felt in letting her family believe she was dead. Someday she hoped to be able to contact them and let them know she was still alive.

Truthfully, she also felt a considerable amount of satisfaction in her domestic accomplishments. Her new life was nothing like she'd imagined.

When she'd decided to marry Nigel, she pictured a life of quiet solitude, one where she had to be vigilant of discovery every second of every day. That had been the case for the first few months. However, over time she had relaxed. And now, in addition to a small but comfortable home, she had a role of prominence in the community and, surprisingly, a few friends.

She also had Nigel.

Heat flooded her cheeks as she thought of her husband. Her marriage was different from others she knew. Though their lives were simple, Moira was happy. More than she had any right to expect.

There was only one thing missing, a secret longing she buried down deep and only acknowledged late at night—once her husband was asleep lying next to her.

She wished Nigel loved her.

No, I don't need that. She already had more than she deserved. Nigel did everything he could to make her feel cared for and protected. And she wasn't some substitute or tool for revenge. Now that she knew him better, it was obvious to her. Nigel had saved her because he was a decent and brave man. He couldn't stand by and watch as others suffered. It was what made him such a skilled minister and an even better husband...although there were many reasons for the latter.

In addition to the thousands of small kindnesses and courtesies he extended to her as his bride, theirs was also passionate union. For a man of the cloth, Nigel was surprisingly carnal—and a generous lover. She had come to enjoy the marriage bed.

Although, enjoy *seems too weak a word for it*, she thought, her body tightening in anticipation when her husband's light step alerted her to his presence.

Nigel's arms came around her, embracing her from behind.

"Hello, wife," he murmured, pressing a hot kiss to her neck, just below her ear.

Reaching up, he fingered a lock of her black hair.

It was one of the safety measures she and Nigel had decided on when they married. He called her Mary in company, and she had darkened her hair with a dye solution of her own creation. More importantly, under her husband's tutelage, she worked at disguising her accent. Since most people this far south had never heard a Scot, she muddled along by staying quiet until she was certain how to pronounce the words she had difficulty with.

"Hello," she whispered huskily when he continued to press kisses down her neck.

She wasn't capable of further speech. He had learned very quickly how to derail her train of thought. But right now they were outside, in full view of anyone that might walk by.

"Um, darling, if you don't want to shock your parishioners, perhaps we should go inside."

Nigel lifted his head. "I'm disappointed you were capable of such a long sentence. You can't usually think when I do that."

She blushed and glanced around, searching for imaginary observers. "It *is* difficult, I assure you. But I don't want you to scandalize your flock and possibly lose your living."

He laughed with a wicked little gleam in his eyes. "Then by all means, let's go inside."

"But the washing—"

Her words were cut off as she was swung bodily up into his arms. Suppressing her naturally loud laughter with a hand over her mouth, she closed her eyes and prayed no one had seen them.

When he carried her into his library, she protested. "Nigel, the maid!"

"I sent her to the village to buy some ink," he said, busy undoing her bodice as he kicked the door closed behind him.

"And the cook?"

"Will stay in the kitchen if she knows what's good for her."

Moira giggled and then sighed as he kissed her. Deciding to help her husband undress, she reached for the placket of his breeches. Her hands were too slow, however, so he tore them open himself before spinning her across the room. Sitting, he urged her down on top of him on the little sofa where he liked to sit and read.

His hands ran up the smooth skin of her legs, moving aside layers of cloth with deft fingers. Teasing and probing, he coaxed her into readiness to receive him. She stared deep into Nigel's eyes as his thick member began to penetrate her slowly from underneath. He had to do it cautiously because, as he teased, the powers that be had been overly generous with his endowments.

She loved watching him possess her. His normally pale cheeks flushed red, and his eyes gleamed like molten silver. Sighing as he slid home, she wrapped her arms around his head as he began to thrust and grind with rough motions that eroded her self-control.

Instinctively she tightened on him, trying to hold on to the tight center of pleasure hidden deep inside her, the one only her husband seemed able to find. He groaned in response, moving his hands to her back. Urged forward with gentle pressure, she closed her eyes in ecstasy when his mouth closed over the swollen tip of her exposed breast.

Heat built on heat and soon she was overcome, weakly holding onto his shoulders as they rocked together in a rhythm older than time. One of his hands moved up to tighten on her waist, and she threw her head back as he laved her nipple in time to his measured thrusts. A few heartbeats later, and she was in paradise.

The helpless flutter of her inner muscles drew Nigel into his own climax. Inside of her, his cock swelled and jerked, spilling his hot seed in powerful bursts that she could feel. The weight and friction of him extended her orgasm, drawing it out until she was drained.

Collapsing against him, she pressed a kiss to his cheek. "Definitely the most wicked clergyman I know."

"Well, I certainly hope so," Nigel teased breathlessly before his playful demeanor fell away.

His hand moved up to trace the soft curve of her cheek. Running an index finger over her full lower lip, he fixed his eyes on hers.

"I love you," he whispered.

Moira gasped, and raised her head to stare down at him, mouth open in shock. Was he serious?

Apparently she was quiet too long because his expression closed up. "It's all right. I don't expect an answer in kind. Perhaps you can let me up. I think I should get back to work on Sunday's service."

She burst into tears.

His brows drew down. "Moira, sweetheart, don't cry," he said, stroking her shoulders.

Covering her hands with her hands, she hastily wiped her tears away.

"I love you, too," she said with a little hiccup.

Amusement crinkled the corners of his lips. "Then why are you crying?"

"Because, I don't deserve you."

Underneath her, he relaxed. "Moira, you deserve the world. I just wish I could give you more—be more for you."

Bending forward, she pressed her forehead to his. "You're everything I need you to be."

THE END

IF YOU ENJOYED this short story, read more about the Spellbound Regency world in Cursed by Lucy Leroux, a Readers' Favorite 5 star read.

Michelle Mollohan for Readers' Favorite wrote:

"Cursed: A Spellbound Regency Novel by Lucy Leroux is a historical romance chock full of magic, curses and drama. Cursed is the second novel I have read by this author. I enjoy her characters, who differ from the typical dynamic of the damsel in distress scenarios found in most romances. She writes vivid lovemaking scenes that fit well into the pace of the story. The added twist of curses and magic made Cursed fun to read from start to finish."

ABOUT THE AUTHOR

Lucy Leroux is another name for USA Today Bestselling Author L.B. Gilbert.

Seven years ago Lucy moved to France for a one-year research contract. Six months later she was living with a handsome Frenchman and is now married with an adorable half-french toddler.

When her last contract ended Lucy turned to writing. Frustrated by a particularly bad romance novel she decided to write her own. Her family lives in Southern California.

Lucy loves all genres of romance and intends to write as many of them as possible. To date she has published twenty plus novels and novellas. These includes paranormal, urban fantasy, gothic regency, and contemporary romances with more on the way. Follow her on twitter or facebook, or check our her website for more news!

www.authorlucyleroux.com